# After All
# Is Said
# & Done

# ANITA DAVIS

ISBN-10: 1-946721-04-2
ISBN-13: 978-1-946721-04-4

Books may be purchased in quantity by contacting the author Anita Davis:
Set Apart Publishing
PO Box 39229
Chicago, IL 60659
or by email at authoranitadavis@gmail.com

# ACKNOWLEDGMENTS

Thank you to all of my family and friends who support me as an author and encourage me daily to pursue my dream of writing.

Thank you to all the people who patiently helped me to choose a new cover for this updated version of this story. And to those who read it before I release it to the public and give me much needed feedback.

A special thanks is extended to my editor, the talented author, Janelle Smith Toussant. You pushed me to do what I know was right, and I thank you for it.

To my readers, thank you for your support this far and I look forward to providing you with countless engaging stories to read.

There is something beautiful about all scars of whatever nature. A scar means the hurt is over, the wound is closed and healed, done with.

*-Harry Crews*

# *1*

"Shhh. We have to be very quiet so that we don't wake your daddy."

"Mommy, where are we going? Is daddy coming too?" Four-year-old Kaylee Rodgers mumbled to her mother. It was three am, and she was not used to being up at that time.

Her father was sound asleep two bedrooms down the hall.

"Shhh. Not now honey. Please put your coat on while I get J.J. dressed."

Two-year-old Jacob Jr. lay fast asleep in his race car bed as his mother bundled him up in his snowsuit.

"Mommy, turn the light on. I can't see. I can't zip my coat."

Carol's hands shook; her heart raced. She struggled to inhale.

"No honey, just do it in the dark."

"Mommy, I can't see."

"Here sweetie, I'll do it."

Kaylee yawned and rubbed her eyes as her mother zipped her coat.

"Mommy, where are we going?"

Carol's mind played tricks on her. Believing that the door knob was turning, she pressed a single finger to Kaylee's lips; a silent plea in her eyes.

Carol grabbed what items she could for the kids, scurried down the stairs and eased out the back door leading to the garage. She rushed to secure the kids in their car seats and locked the doors to her BMW four-matic. When the garage door was completely open, she paused and leaned against the headrest. She heaved a sigh of relief.

There was pounding. The car shook. "Carol, what are you doing? Please don't leave! Don't take my kids away from me."

Her husband, Jacob Sr., stood barefoot in the garage screaming. His face was laced with sorrow, but he continued to pound furiously on the driver's side window. It was like the car was no match for his monstrous frame. At six-two and two-hundred and twenty pounds of lean muscle, Jacob was more than the average man.

Beads of sweat trickled down Carol's face as her clammy hands gripped the steering wheel. Kaylee screamed and covered her ears.

"Kaylee honey, it's okay. Mommy's not taking you anywhere."

Carol, with her swollen and discolored left eye, turned towards the driver's side window to face her husband. "Shut up Jacob! Just shut up!"

"Carol baby, we can work this out."

"Work this out? Do you see my eye? I think my ribs are broken, and you're saying we can work this out."

She had to leave him. She determined that his empty promises to change would not be the death of her.

\*\*\*

"So when will we tell them?" Michele whined into the phone.

"Soon enough, but just not now." *How long can I continue to keep this from Carol?*

"Bye. I'll talk to you soon." He needed another cold one after that conversation. Distraught, he dropped the phone in his lap and rubbed his face in angst before he finally took the keys out of the ignition. He drug his feet as he entered his house through the garage.

Lately, Jacob had been coming home around eight p.m., way past the time he got off work, drunk.

"Where is my food?" He directed his question at his wife Carol who was busying herself in the kitchen as he walked towards the den. "Look at this house. You call this clean?" He wiped at an end table searching for dust and found some. He shook his head. "You're at home all day and you can't even keep the house clean. I just don't know what to say about you." He was like the character Two-Face in the Batman movie; one man composed of opposing creatures dwelling inside, good and evil. Jacob was loving when he was not intoxicated. He used to praise everything she did. Showered her with compliments on how smart and beautiful she was. He never raised his voice and was affectionate towards her. However, since he began drinking, Carol just could not seem to do anything right around the house. If he was not berating her about how awful he thought her cooking was, then it was about how unkempt he thought she was keeping the house. His patience with her had become short.

Carol made it clear from the beginning of their courtship how she desired to be treated by Jacob. He knew what her mom had gone through at the hands of her dad and vowed he would never be that way to her. She could not understand where his recent change of behavior came from. The late night drinking spells made him mirror an evil mad man destined to destroy whatever was in his path; except for his kids. He loved his kids, which was a part of his current dilemma.

While Jacob was busy ranting, Carol rushed to fix his plate. Breathing a long sigh, she paused at the kitchen entryway and whispered, "Lord, please let there be peace in our home tonight."

Carol plastered a smile on her face as she re-entered the den. "Here, I made your favorite, steak and potatoes."

"Hmph, who said this is my favorite? It was dry and bland last time."

Her lips remained tight as she rushed to get him a cold glass of water. She returned and handed him the cup.

"I don't want water, I want a beer."

Sensing he had drunk too much already; she just stood there.

"Why are you still standing here? I said bring me a beer."

"We're out of beer," she said avoiding eye contact with him.

"We are, are we? I just bought a case in here yesterday." He jumped out of his seat sending food flying everywhere. "Move out of my way." Brown juice from the steak splattered the tan rug.

He growled and pushed her aside. Jacob stormed into the kitchen and flung open the refrigerator practically tearing the door off its hinges. Right where he left it, the unopened case of beer lay on the bottom shelf. He slowly turned around. His pupils danced. His nostrils flared. He spoke with a surprisingly tempered voice. "Why would you lie to me? You think I'm stupid?"

"No…no…no…" Carol whispered as tears rolled down her cheeks. She slowly backed away from his advancing steps. If he did hit her, it would be the third time since he started drinking. With each time, he became more and more violent. She just couldn't figure out where his sudden desire to be physically abusive to her came from.

The first time he slapped her so hard that it sent her five foot five, 115 pound petite frame careening to the floor. The second time he left so many bruises on her arms and back that she was grateful for the cold Illinois winters. The brisk winds helped her to hide all the bruises under long sleeve shirts. But this time she saw such rage in his eyes that she did not know what would become of her if he hit her. He continued to move towards her. "I'm sorry Jacob. I didn't know there was any beer left, I swear I didn't know."

"Yes, you did. I bet you've been in and out of the refrigerator all day. You knew it was there." His eyes seemed to change to a shade of fiery orange-red as he reached out to grab her throat. She escaped his grip and ran through the family room towards the stairs leading up to the children's room. He never hit her in front of the kids. If she could make it to the kids' room, she thought she might escape his wrath.

She sprinted to the stairs hoping to take double steps to get to the top quicker, but she felt her head jerk back as he wrapped her long black hair around his fist. He snatched her back down to the floor.

"Jacob, no. Please don't." She screamed and kicked as he dragged her back through the family room towards the kitchen. Desperate to stop him from dragging her, she reached out for anything she could hold on to, but his massive frame was just too much for her to overcome.

"You, of all people, lie to me," Jacob sputtered. He pounded on Carol's face. She tried to shield it with the kitchen floor. Whenever she tried to cover her face, he jabbed her in her ribs. So many things went through his mind as he pounded on her body. After the first two blows, it was not Carol he was hitting on, but every bit of bad news he was given the last two months. It wasn't until he heard the muffled blood-filled moans from her mouth that he realized it was his wife's limp body that lay beneath him.

"Carol? Carol? Wake up," he shouted, hoping that she wasn't dead. Realizing what he had done, he stood up and backed away from her only to slide down the wall to the floor and bury his head in between his legs in shame. With his head low, he spoke loudly, "Carol baby, I'm sorry, I lost it again. I lost it again…" The more he said "I lost it" the closer he tried to get to her to comfort her.

Face scrunched and eyes like daggers she screamed with all the strength she could muster up. "Get away…get away…get away."

He stood and looked down at his wife, noticing just how badly he had beat her. His pulse quickened. He punched holes in the walls and smashed the mirrors as he retreated upstairs to their master bedroom.

Carol lay limp on the kitchen floor for what seemed like hours. Moving was painful for her. For the life of her, she couldn't understand what triggered her husband's rage yet again. Struggling to her feet, she realized that her face had to be so swollen that it caused her left eye to shut. She kept her head low and turned off all of the lights to avoid seeing herself in what was left of the mirrors on the wall along the way to the stairs.

She noticed the trail of blood on the tan carpet that hugged the stairs as she walked them. She knew whose it was and did not care if he was in pain or not. She wanted to get in the tub to soak her sore body in hot water as she did before.

She did not go to the bathroom in their bedroom, but rather the guest bathroom on the other end of the hallway. She finally looked at herself in the mirror. Tears welled up in her eyes as she stood there looking at her bloody swollen face in the mirror. Once the tub was full, she eased into the water until it touched her chin.

Her bath water soon turned to salt water from the pool of tears she cried. She thought back to the many times in her childhood she watched her father beat her mother. She wondered how she allowed herself to get to where she was at that point; a place she swore she would never be, a victim of domestic violence.

She was twelve when she finally worked up the nerve to ask her mother why she stayed with her dad in spite of how he was. Her mother averted eye contact with her but spoke frankly, "I'll do anything to make sure that you and your brother are taken care of. If that means I have to take a few beatings every now and then to keep your father around, I'll do it. Aside from the abuse, he's a good man. He has never cheated on me, he keeps a roof over our heads, clothes on our backs, and plenty of food to eat." Those words always rang in Carol's head as a sign of a weak woman rather than one who would do things on her own before she allowed a man to abuse her. Her father's treatment of her mother kept Carol determined not to be with a man like her father.

Meeting Jacob seemed like heaven to her. He never disrespected her with his words or actions. When they were in college, he had the rookies on the team to deliver the letters to her dorm room that he wrote weekly, if not daily. He was always gentle with her so when he asked her to marry him two years after they graduated and were settled into their careers; she was elated. He was vice president of a lucrative marketing firm in downtown Chicago while Carol was a kindergarten teacher in a northern suburb. Jacob knew Carol wanted to work in spite of how much money he earned, and it did not bother him that she wanted to keep her identity as a teacher. However, years into their marriage Carol had Kaylee and decided to be a stay-at-home mom. She was all the more comfortable with that decision when she had Jacob Jr. two years later. Carol admired the life they had built for themselves and their kids until about two months prior when she noticed a drastic change in his evening behavior and demeanor.

Carol realized that she must have been sitting in the now chilled water for such a long time, that it caused her pale skin to become excessively wrinkly. She continued to sit there and ponder her next move. She dried off, contemplating where she would sleep for the night. She figured her head would be clearer in the morning. She did not want to make any rash decisions at that point. She went to the guest bedroom, pulled back the soft duvet, and climbed into the cold lonely queen-sized bed to lay her head on the pillow.

She jumped up.

The feeling of what it would be like to lie on sharp broken glass stung her left side kept her from getting comfortable. *Are my ribs broken?*

Her body ached. Her face was swollen. She really did love Jacob, but if he beat her like that this particular night, there was no telling if she would survive another time. She quietly rushed from the guest room into the bedroom shared by the kids to get them dressed.

The nightlight was on in the kids' room and she turned it off not wanting Kaylee to see her. The soft stream of moonlight peeking through the window would have to suffice as she dressed the kids.

She could not afford for Kaylee to see her distorted face.

\*\*\*

She turned the car on. "Jacob. I can't do this anymore. Get out of the way." Carol tried to scream as loud as she could through the pain of her swollen jaw. She put the car in drive.

By now Jacob was kneeling in a praying position in the snow in the middle of the driveway. "Carol,

I'm so sorry honey. Please forgive me. I'll get help. I can stop this. I promise I can. Just come back in and put the kids back to bed. We can work this out. Let's talk about this. Please…"

She ignored his plea. He had sworn to her the last two times that he would never do it again. She swerved around him in the driveway and onto the street. She sped away.

After minutes of kneeling in the driveway and several inquiries from his awakened neighbors questioning stares, Jacob went back into the house and sat in the bloody spot where his wife lay earlier that night.

# *2*

Carol drove with no exact destination in mind. It did not make sense to her to go to her parents' house because when she spoke to her mother about the other two times, her mom told her everything would be okay. She knew that if she showed up there her mother would readily defend Jacob and encourage her to go back home. She recalled the last time she ran to her mother for safety after Jacob's abuse.

*"Here's some ice for your arm since you refuse to soak in a tub of it. I'm telling you the soreness and pain will go away in no time if you heed my*

*advice." Edith spoke as she watered the plants resting on the windowsill in the bay window of her kitchen.*

*"Mom, if it were up to you, Jacob could beat me senseless and I shouldn't complain or be unhappy." She shifted in her seat to ease the tension of its high back on her bruised back.*

*"No honey, I don't wish pain on you. I just..."*
*Edith hated seeing her daughter follow in her*
*footsteps of accepting abuse from their husbands,*
*but how could she encourage her daughter to*
*walk away when she never had the courage to do*
*so?*

Carol feared going to her older brother Mark's
house would send him rushing back to her house to
inflict the same or worse amount of pain onto Jacob.
The only other person she could think to turn to was
her best friend, Sheila.

\*\*\*

Sheila rolled over to the snores of her latest
rendezvous, Damien. All six feet of him laid there
almost naked except for the checkered cotton boxers
rumpled up against his smooth pecan skin. His pecks
jumped as he rolled over.

Sheila did not mean for him to fall asleep in her
bed, but he handled his business so well with her
earlier that night that she figured she could at least
let him sleep a little longer before she put him out.

No man was allowed to spend the night.

She did not want them thinking that their one
night of bliss would lead to anything long term. She
arched her back, licked her lips, and her temperature

rose as she thought about all of the things he did to her that night.

She was tempted to wake him up for another round of sex, but when she inhaled a whiff of his latest bout of flatulence, she was turned off. She looked at the clock on her nightstand; it read 4:10 am. She would let him sleep for another half-hour before she put him out. He couldn't still be there when the sun rose.

She rolled on her side thinking about the many sleepless nights she had. No matter how many sleeping pills she took or how many men she satisfied in bed, she could never blot out the images of what happened to her in her childhood. *Why didn't anyone ever stop it? Didn't momma know what was happening to me?* Her questions always made her reach for a cigarette. She lit it and pulled on it for a long time before she exhaled the circles that she could form with the smoke. The cigarettes, and being around her godchildren, were the only things that seemed to silence her past.

Sheila tossed the butt of the cigarette into the ashtray on her nightstand. She was tired of Damien still lying next to her. "Hey. You've got to go." She rolled him over and out of the bed. His massive body made a loud thump when he hit the floor. She got up from the bed, grabbed her robe, and gathered his belongings.

"Whoa…" Disoriented and struggling to see in the dark, Damien stumbled to his feet.

"I said, you've got to go." Sheila spoke sternly as she shoved his things into his arms and pushed him towards the door.

"What? You're kicking me out? I thought we had a good time last night?"

"We did, and now it's over."

His chipped tooth beamed as he smiled at her.

"I'll call you soon." She lied.

"Well ain't this something. Normally I'm the one to love em' and leave em', but here I am getting kicked out in the wee hours of the morning." He laughed as she pushed him further towards the door. He practically had to hop into his pants and boots.

Sheila continued to escort him down the stairs.

"So when can I see you again?"

"I said that I would call you soon."

"Are you sure? I definitely want to see you again. You know exactly what to do, and you do it so well." He licked his lips. "You're pretty too."

"Do you understand English or not? I said I would call you." Sheila huffed and shoved him out the front door.

The door did not close. His foot held it open. He grinned. "Can I get a kiss before I leave?"

She smirked and beckoned him to her with her pointer finger.

She grabbed him by his shirt collar and pulled him even closer. She stared into his eyes.

He licked his lips.

"Kiss the door." She pushed him back and slammed the door in his face. "I won't be calling him. He's too clingy, and only after one night. It was our first time, but it'll certainly be the last." She went back upstairs to her bedroom to change her sheets. She showered, laid down and closed her eyes trying to get some sleep before she had to get ready for work.

# *3*

Carol made a right onto Sheila's street and within seconds pulled into her friend's driveway. Jacob Jr. had slept through all of the commotion and Kaylee cried herself to sleep sometime after Carol left her house. The sun was nowhere near rising when Carol rang Sheila's doorbell.

"Who could be at my door this time of the morning? It better not be that fool. I don't care what he left, he won't be getting it." Sheila raced down her curved staircase to the door. The incessant bird-chirping-hum of her doorbell worked her already frayed nerves. She wanted to snatch the door open, but decided to see who was out there first. She looked through the peep hole but did not recognize the petite woman. A little bit more at ease with a woman's presence at her door, instead of Damien having come back, her chest deflated as she exhaled deeply. Sheila slowly eased the gigantic wooden door open.

Wide-eyed, Sheila gasped, "Oh my God!" She slowly covered her mouth. She reached out to embrace Carol. Sheila's response made Carol realize how bad she must have looked. She sank to the ground weeping.

"Carol honey, what happened to you? Oh my God." Sheila frantically waved for Carol to come inside.

Carol stammered through her tears trying to control herself. "Sheila…I need to get the kids out of the car, can you help me?"

"Don't worry, I'll get them, you just go on in the den and lie down." Sheila power-walked to the car with her silk floral robe flapping in the wind and grabbed J.J. from his booster seat. Luckily she had a room on the first floor that she turned into the kids' room after she was deemed their godmother. She placed him in his race car bed that was identical to the one he had at home. She rushed back out to get Kaylee and put her in her little princess bed with a life-size crown for a headboard. After undressing the kids and tucking them in, Sheila softly closed the door and headed to the den.

"Carol sweetheart, what happened?" Sheila could tell that Carol had been beaten badly she was just not clear by whom.

Carol and Sheila had been best friends since freshman year in high school. They did everything together and went everywhere together, so it was no surprise to either of their families when they decided they would go off to the same college together, Clark Atlanta. Carol was ready to dig into her major, elementary education, but Sheila was ready to dig into the guys on campus, although she was very studious as well. She majored in communications with an emphasis in public relations; a major that she thought gave her the license to be vocal with anyone she came in contact with.

Sheila first caught the eye of the star quarterback on the football team. Her sassy pixie haircut, smooth mocha skin, and Coca-Cola bottle shaped frame made her a front runner for one of his latest conquests, but little did he know that he was on her radar. They hooked up immediately and sought each other out sexually as desired.

Sheila wanted Carol to loosen up more and enjoy college, so she asked the quarterback to hook her friend up with a nice guy. He introduced Sheila to Jacob. After weeks of sizing up and drilling Jacob, Sheila felt like he was worthy of Carol's attention. She introduced the two, and it was love, at first sight.

Before long, the quarterback was completely out of the picture and as the years progressed Carol, Jacob, and Sheila were the best of friends. Sheila even helped Jacob plan his proposal to Carol, helped Carol plan the wedding, was the maid of honor, and the godmother of their children. As the years went on, the bond between the three knitted stronger. Sheila considered Carol to be her sister and Jacob was like her big brother.

It never crossed her mind that it could have been her brother's hands, Jacob's hands, which had transformed Carol's butterscotch freckled skin into black, blue, and puffy masses. Sheila came back to the present moment at the sound of Carol's whimpering voice.

"Jacob. I didn't want to tell you before because I foolishly thought that it wouldn't happen again, but this was the third and the last time. I won't be like my mother," Carol spoke as she put her head down and sobbed.

# *4*

Jacob barely got any sleep when he went back in the house. He kept replaying the night over and over in his head. He knew he messed up this time, but he would do whatever it took to get his wife and kids back.

He got into bed and dozed off. He was having a nightmare, and it interrupted him from getting much-needed sleep. It starred a gruesome character, him, and a beautiful woman being destroyed by his hands and actions. He woke up screaming out his apologies to Carol. His eyes were heavy, and they burned as he tried to block the images out of his head. The sheets were covered with sweat as he wrestled with himself trying to erase the memories of what he had done to his wife, to his family. Exhaustion finally grabbed hold of him, and he fell asleep.

He awoke a few hours later wanting to find Carol and straighten things out. The first place he went to was Carol's parents' house. He put on his poker face. He breathed deep, calming himself down before he entered their home. "Hi mom, hi dad," he said as he closed the door behind him.

"Hello, Jacob my boy. Looks like you had a rough night," Edgar, Carol's father, retorted sitting in his usual spot with a beer in his hand and his eyes barely looking up from the TV.

"Yeah, sort of. How are you doing?" His eyes searched the parts of the house he could see from his seat on the couch. He was looking for signs of Carol or the kids being there.

"Same ole, same ole." Edgar sipped on his beer.

Jacob wrung his hands together. "Hey dad, do you know where Carol and the kids are?"

Edith walked in the room. "No, we haven't heard from her…Why don't you know where she is?" Carol's mom laughed with a raised eyebrow.

Jacob sat up straight. "Oh, now I remember, Kaylee had a doctor's appointment. Well, I have to go. See y'all." Jacob bolted towards the door to avert any further questions from his mother-in-law. He rushed to his car and jumped in. He sat there watching his breath fog up the windows completely before he finally decided to turn the car on. He was not ready to stop looking for Carol and the kids that day.

Jacob drove past Sheila's house, but there was no sign of Carol being there.

He did not have a job to go to, so he headed home. He parked his car and entered the house the same way he did the night before, only this time there was no wife there to greet him. All he saw was dried blood on the floor and shattered glass lining the hallway.

He went to the pantry to get cleaning supplies to clean the mess he made. He thought about the night before and his actions and he was infuriated all over again. He grabbed plates out the cabinets and smashed them to the floor.

Moments passed, and it seemed as if he had managed to break every single dish they owned, but his rage was not over. He remembered there was chinaware in the dining room. He headed there and tore the room apart, smashing everything he could pick up into tiny pieces.

He did not stop there. He searched for things to destroy in the den. He picked up the first thing he saw, but fell to the ground sobbing as he looked at it. It was a framed Christmas card from last year of Carol, him, and the kids. *Carol. My kids. I can't live without them.* Exhaustion became his companion again and he fell asleep on the den floor clutching the picture of his family.

He managed to sleep until evening. His back was stiff from being balled up in a fetal position on the floor. He rose to his feet and stretched tall and wide as he tried to gather his wits about what had happened. He retraced his steps back through the house to the kitchen. Not only was his wife's dried blood still there as a reminder of how stupid he had behaved, but there was now shattered glass everywhere that he would have to clean up.

He was not in the mood to clean, and although he had slept, he had not gotten rest, so he retreated upstairs to his room and wrestled with the nightmare he inflicted upon Carol. For the next couple of days, his day consisted of looking for his family during the day and restless nights of longing for Carol and his kids.

Jacob woke up one morning days after Carol had left with the kids. His lips were cracked from dehydration and his stomach ached with hunger. He went to the kitchen with the intentions of finally eating after days of non-intentional fasting and the sight of his wife's blood and broken dishes everywhere quickened his will to get his family back. *Yes, I have to clean up. I have to have the house perfect for when Carol and the kids come back home. Things will be different when she comes back.*

*I'll show her. I'll spend the rest of my life making it up to her.*

Jacob seemed to have a renewed hope in what would become of him and Carol once she returned home. *My phone.* Jacob patted himself down. *Let me find my phone and check to see if I missed any calls from Carol.*

He found his phone but it was dead.

He located his charger in the den and plugged up the phone. After it was powered on, he smiled at the thought of hearing Carol's voice in a message, but his smile turned into a scowl when he saw that the only missed calls he had, thirty to be exact, had come from Michele. He did not have time to deal with her. This time he would not let anger get the best of him. He went back to the pantry and grabbed what he needed to clean the mess he made.

He tried to remain hopeful about getting Carol back, but how could he when he could not even find her. His search for Carol had taken a toll on him. He knew she was not at her parents' home. He did not think she was at Sheila's either because he had driven past her house several times to no avail.

He was not bold enough yet to go knock on Sheila's door. Sheila was feisty, and if she had any knowledge of what occurred between him and Carol, he was sure that Sheila's response to him would not be so pleasant. Sheila was like a sister to him, but he knew his bond with her did not compare to the one she had with Carol.

Out of options as to where she could be and knowing that they kept a very small circle of friends, Jacob decided to swing by Carol's brother's house to see if she was there or had been by during the week.

Jacob had a good relationship with Carol's brother, but that and the cold winter winds did not stop his hands from clamming up as he rang the doorbell.

"Who is it?" Mark called out from the computer table in the dining room.

"It's me Jacob."

"Oh, hey J. Give me a second." Mark opened the door and embraced his brother-in-law in a bear hug.

Jacob had not seen him in a while. With such a cordial invite into the house, Jacob figured that Mark must have not known what happened. So instead of discussing Carol's whereabouts and raising Mark's suspicions, Jacob pretended he just stopped by to check up on Mark.

"So what brings you by Mr. Executive Man?" Mark, blue collar man, always ragged on Jacob's white collar persona.

"Oh nothing, haven't seen you in a while, just stopping through to check up on you."

"Everything's cool. Ellen is due any day now with our first baby. I'm just trying to catch up with you and Carol." Mark laughed. He stood up shoulder to shoulder with Jacob and playfully slapped him on the back.

"Well, like I said, I just stopped by to say hi, but I have to go now."

"Hey, is everything alright? I've been calling you all for the last couple of days, and it's going straight to voicemail and mom said she hasn't talked to Carol in days either."

"Yeah, everything's cool. Just a little trouble with incoming calls, but I called the phone company today, and they promised to have it fixed by tomorrow, or we'll just have to get new phones. I'll tell Carol to call you soon. Okay bye, have a good evening."

"Bye Jacob, and kiss my niece and nephew for me."

By the time Jacob got back to his car, tears had escaped his eyes and streamed down his face. He thought of not having kissed his kids goodnight for the past week. Even though he had called Sheila and had been to her house every day since Carol left, he figured going by there one more time could not hurt.

\*\*\*

Not knowing that Jacob would try coming back again so soon after having lurked outside for hours every other day that week, Carol thought it would be okay to leave her SUV in the driveway for a while after she had come back from the grocery store.

Jacob sat in his parked car down the street from Sheila's house. He watched Carol take the groceries in the house nearly an hour ago. She tried carrying all of the bags in at one time, but after a few attempts of trying to gather them all, she settled on making two trips to get all of the bags in the house. He desperately wanted to help her, hold her, but he sat frozen in the car deciding what he would say when he finally got the nerve to go up to the house. He rubbed the stubble on his face, smiling at the possibility of seeing her up close and hugging his kids soon. He exhaled loudly looking into the mirror at the dark circles under his eyes. He put his skull cap on and pulled his key from the ignition.

His steps felt like he was walking in wet cement as he made his way to Sheila's front door. He heard the faint sound of laughter coming from the back of the house near the kitchen. Instead of knocking on the door or ringing the bell as he had wanted to do all week, he walked around to the back of the house. There was no denying Carol's existence there as he stood on the patio looking into the kitchen.

Carol was still grieved by what happened with Jacob over the past two months and especially his violent behavior earlier that week, but Sheila had succeeded in at least making Carol laugh, reminiscing about better days when they were younger. Carol's joy turned into a mixture of fear and hate running through her veins when she turned from closing the refrigerator door to look out onto the patio and see Jacob standing there.

Carol shrieked. "What is he doing here Sheila?" She ran from the kitchen into the room where the kids were playing and locked the door. Kaylee ran to her mother.

"Mommy, what's wrong? Are you okay? What's wrong with your face?"

"Nothing. Everything is okay. Everything is okay angel." She kissed the top of Kaylee's forehead. "Go back to playing with your brother."

Carol sat on the floor with her back against the door. She had avoided the kids seeing her face until the swelling went down, and most of the bruising went away, but it was difficult to hide from them because her kids were used to seeing her all day every day.

Since the incident, she spoke to them from behind a door or with her back to them. Today was the first day the children saw her face. Still bruised enough to cause Kaylee to know that her mommy had been hurt, but in no way as disfigured as it was when she first arrived at Sheila's house.

\*\*\*

"You have a lot of nerve showing up here day after day as if you've done nothing wrong. I can't believe I'm the one that actually introduced you to her. I looked up to you like you were my brother." Sheila's mouth tightened; she shook her head. "I was only following Carol's request of not answering the door or my phone, but I know what you did and let me just say that I hope you get run over by a semi-truck at full speed. You worthless piece of...breathe Sheila, just breath. Don't go there with him," Sheila talked out loud trying to calm herself down.

The winter chill in the air did not faze her at all. Had it been four years ago, Sheila would have used every obscenity imaginable to tell Jacob just how she truly felt at that moment, but ever since Kaylee was born, she tried hard not to use foul language.

"Sheila I know I deserve everything you're saying to me, and more." His eyes softened. "I'm still your brother."

Sheila's eyes bucked as she rolled her neck.

"There is nothing that I could possibly say to excuse my behavior. I know I was out of line."

"Oh, I call almost beating your wife to a pulp more than out of line."

"You're right," he paused, "but this is something between me and Carol. I need to talk to my wife." He stepped forward.

Sheila reached for a knife in the cutlery rack on the island.

Jacob stepped back.

"You had better stay back, because if you inch up again, I'll be the one explaining to the cops how I stabbed you in self-defense." Sheila stood in the doorway with one hand on her hip and the other gripping a carving knife.

"Will you at least hear me out?"

Sheila pursed her lips.

"Some months ago my company went bankrupt. There was nothing left to get, no pension, no 401K, nothing." Jacob talked nervously as he sweated in the cold. "Even our life insurance policies were null and void."

"And so you think your little sob story gives you license to pound on your wife?" Sheila asked, not in the least bit touched by his story.

Judging Sheila's mood, he figured he better not share the news of Michele and his twins just yet.

Sheila pretended to play an imaginary violin.

"Me not being able to provide for my family reminded me too much of my worthless father. I tried to get another job, but no one would hire me. I tapped out what we had in our savings trying to keep the bills current."

Sheila shook her head in disgust.

"It all was too much for me. I started drinking." Jacob tried to lighten up the mood. "Come on Sheila, you know I can't hold liquor. Remember that one time in college you came and picked me up from that bar after the team lost the championship?"

"Mmmm hmmmm." Sheila pursed her lips and rolled her eyes.

"Remember I was too embarrassed to call Carol so I called you?"

"I said I do." Sheila crossed her arms.

"Remember the bartender told you I only had three shots that night?" Jacob looked into Sheila's eyes but saw no empathy for him, he continued to speak. "You were there for me like you've always been there for me and I've always appreciated that." Jacob smiled faintly trying to soften Sheila's demeanor.

Her nostrils flared, and her eyes narrowed in on him.

"Come on now Sheila, you saw how I was with just three drinks. I hate to admit it, but I would have twice as much as that before I made it home to Carol." Jacob shook his head. "I drank to bury my problems but ended up taking my frustrations out on Carol." Jacob lowered his head.

"So let me get this straight, you don't have a job and you've wiped out your savings account?"

"Yeah." Jacob sighed.

"And your dumb ass didn't think that with a master's degree and all your experience that you couldn't easily get another job, take out a loan, hell, tell your wife? Darn-it, see, look what you've done, you've made me curse," Sheila spoke as the knife flailed in her hand.

"I didn't know what to do but drink. It made me feel better, numb. I didn't tell Carol because I didn't want her to worry. I thought I could get everything under control, but I guess I couldn't. I know I was wrong, but it wasn't until I would hear her scream or cry out that I would realize what I had done. I know I messed up, that's why I'm here trying to make things right."

"I'm still not touched Jacob." She waved the knife dismissively at him. "You and Carol had too great of a marriage to ruin it the way you did. The swelling on her face is just now starting to go down and did you know that you broke three of her ribs? You hear me, three. I hope you don't expect her to forgive you."

Jacob put his head down in shame.

"Sheila, I can talk for myself now." Carol had been listening at the kitchen door the whole time.

The sight of Carol's healing face hurt him more than any of them imagined it ever could. He forgot Sheila's threat; he tried to enter the house again.

"Didn't I already tell you what I'd do to you if you moved this way again?" She stood flat-footed daring him to move again.

He believed her threats. He saw the worry in Carol's eyes and backed up even more.

Carol came closer to the patio door as she spoke. "If only you would have seen me the morning after you beat me then you would have really seen what you did to me." She raised her voice, "or if you would have sat there as the x-ray machine displayed my broken ribs. Or just maybe seeing me avoid the kids these past days so they wouldn't see what their father did to their mother."

Jacob dropped to his knees, but Carol continued to speak, ignoring him. "Maybe then you would begin to understand what you've put me...the kids...no, all of us through. I heard everything you said to Sheila. Obviously you didn't trust me enough to share what was going on, so that means that I can't trust you to trust me. I can't trust you to keep your hands off of me."

"Yes, you can baby."

"Shut up. I'm talking now." Carol was finding her voice. "You've known all along that I would never be like my mother, and stick around an abusive husband, but like a fool I forgave you the first time you slapped me and then the next time when you bruised every part of me but my face, but the third time was the last time. I will not be your punching bag Jacob, do you hear me? I will not be your punching bag!"

"Carol, I'm sorry baby. Please forgive me." Jacob jumped to his feet. "We can work this out. I swear I'll never do it again. Just give us another chance." Jacob stood frozen on the patio. Not from the below zero wind-chilled air grazing his face, but from the cold empty stare in Carol's eyes as she looked into his.

"Jacob, it's over." She turned and walked out of the kitchen.

"Goodbye," Sheila said as she closed the door in his face. She closed the drapes.

# *5*

Michele sat alone in her room at her parents' house while the twins were at her brother's house playing with his children. She hated the strain her secret had on her relationship with her brother in the past. He was best friends with Jacob, but she was his sister, so Michael kept her secret. They argued often over the years because of Michele's obsession with Jacob. She hounded Michael to give her details of Jacob's life as the years went by. Michael ignored her as much as he could concerning the matter, but Michele always had a cunning way of getting what she wanted.

She hated not being able to be with Jacob. He was her high school crush. She was smitten by him from the moment her brother introduced them.

*"Mom! Can you get Michele? She won't leave me and Jacob alone." Michael pushed his younger*

ANITA DAVIS

*sister towards the door, but she wouldn't leave out. "Get out. You annoying twerp." Michael flopped back down on his bed and picked up his controller to the game.*

*"Michael, it's okay. We're just playing the game. She's not bothering us." Jacob winked at Michele.*

*"See, dork." Michele popped Michael in the back of the head and sat down next to Jacob, "I'm not annoying." She stuck her tongue out at him.*

*"No, you're cool." Jacob let his knee fall against Michele's.*

*Her breathing became uneven and she blushed. She ran out of the room before he could see just how red her face had become. She would be sure to be calmer and even more appealing the next time he came around.*

She made sure she was around whenever Jacob came over. He was her first real love, her first everything. Although they were young when they were together, he had a lasting hold on her heart.

It was her Aunt Tammy that had convinced her all of those years to leave things be where she and Jacob were concerned, but now that she was back in the Chicagoland area she would do whatever she could to get him back.

She had been pressuring Jacob about finally introducing him to the twins as their father and spending more time with them. She hated how he would rush her off the phone right before he entered the home he shared with Carol. Carol. She cursed the day Carol was born. How could she like the woman that stood in between her happiness with Jacob?

She went to the kitchen to pour herself another glass of red wine. It had become her companion since she returned home. Her thoughts of being with Jacob consumed her more now than ever, and Pinot Noir seemed to be the only thing putting her at ease until they could be together as a family. Just thinking about him made her reach out to grab her phone and call him. His phone rang and rang. "Hello, you've reached Jacob Rodgers. I'm unable to take your call at the moment, but if you leave your name, number, and a brief message, I'll be sure to return your call at my earliest convenience."

"Jacob," she cooed into the phone, "it's me Michele. I haven't heard from you in a couple of days. I just want to talk to you…about the boys. Call me back when you get this message. Talk to you soon."

She pressed the end button and dropped her phone on her bed since she was back in her room. She was tired of waiting for Jacob to figure out how he would tell his wife. *I don't care about Carol's feelings. I just want me, Jacob, and the boys to be a family. It's my turn to be happy, with Jacob. Since he's taking his time ending things between them, I'll just have to speed things up.*

She reached for her phone again and scrolled through her contacts looking for the number. She had managed to get Carol's number from Jacob's phone the last time he came over and left his phone on the coffee table when he went to the bathroom. She clicked on the envelope icon under Carol's name. She typed in the box: *I'm his first, and I'll be his last.* Michele pressed send and fell back on her bed in laughter. She hoped her message would cause Carol to question Jacob's fidelity and put stress on their marriage.

She had no idea what was going on with Jacob and Carol at the moment.

# *6*

"Edith." Edgar called to the back. "Have you talked to Carol? Seems like we haven't seen or heard from her all week long."

"What did you say?" Edith walked into the living room drying her hands with a dish towel.

"I asked if you'd heard from Carol. I haven't seen my grands all week long. I miss them and Carol."

"Come to think of it, I haven't heard from her this week. I've tried calling her a couple of times, and it went straight to her voicemail each time. She hasn't called back, but I guess we shouldn't worry because Jacob stopped by earlier this week, and he didn't mention that anything was wrong. Oh wait, remember he told us that something was wrong with their phones, but it should be fixed soon."

"Phone or no phone, she normally doesn't let this long go by without stopping by to see us and bringing the grands over."

"Well honey, you know Carol and Jacob always have lots of things going on with the kids. Maybe they are just caught up in their plans with them."

"Give me the phone. I'll call her." Edgar held his hand out knowing that Edith would be swift to place it in his hands.

"Here. I hope she answers it, so you can calm down and stop worrying." Edith hummed and walked back into the kitchen.

Edgar let the phone ring and just when he was about to hang up he heard the faint voice of his daughter.

"Hi, dad." A tear seeped from Carol's eye recalling that she had not seen her dad in a week. He may not have been a good husband, but he was a great father to her.

"Carol, baby, how are you? What have you been up to? We haven't heard from you all week. I miss you and the grands."

"Hold on dad." Carol checked her text message alert to see that an unknown number had texted her, it read: *Enjoy him while you still have him because your time with him will end soon.* There was a winking emoticon at the end of the message. Carol shook her head as she heard her father call her name on the phone.

"Carol. Carol."

"Yeah dad, I'm uh…" Carol was still reeling from the text she just read. She ignored her dad's questions.

"Carol, what's wrong? Is everything ok? You know that you can talk to me about anything right?"

"Dad. Jacob-"

"Jacob what?"

"He, he hit me…" Carol patted her eye trying to feel if the swelling was gone, like the trust she had in Jacob.

"He did what?" Edgar swung his feet from the ottoman and sat up straight in his chair as fast as he could.

"He came in the house drunk one night…he, he, he broke a few of my ribs and left my face black and blue." She cried.

Edgar jumped up out of his seat and roared. "I'll kill him!"

Edith rushed into the living room. "Edgar, what is it?"

"Jacob. He hurt my little girl. I'm gonna kill him!" Edgar paced the floor as fast as he could at his age. "Are you okay sweetie? Where is he? Where are you? Are my grandkids okay? Don't tell me that you're still at that house with him."

Edgar asked the questions faster than Carol could answer them.

Edith reached out to get the phone from Edgar. "Calm down, calm down Edgar. This has happened before, and Carol was alright. Let me speak to her."

Edgar turned his head at neck breaking speed to face Edith. "What? This happened before?"

"Yes." Edith lowered her head.

"You mean you knew he's been hurting my little girl, and you never told me about it?" Edgar's blood pressure rose.

Edith managed to pry the phone out of Edgar's hands to speak with Carol. "Carol, are you okay? Come over. I'll take care of you."

"Mom, I'm not coming over. You'll just try to convince me to stay with Jacob. He and I are through. I will not be his punching bag, and I will not allow my kids to grow up thinking it's okay for their father to beat their mother."

A tear fell from Edith's eye. "Carol we've had this conversation before. I told you why I did what I did." Edith inwardly cursed herself for what her daughter was going through. "Carol just please come over. I'm here for you."

Edgar grabbed the phone from Edith. She retreated to the kitchen. "Carol, you aren't still in the house with him, are you?"

"No dad, I'm not."

"Good. Well, where are you?"

"I'm safe. The kids are safe. We're staying with a friend." She did not want them to know that she was staying with Sheila. They knew where Sheila lived and would rush over.

"A friend. What friend, Sheila?"

"No, dad." Carol lied.

"We're family. Come be with us. We're here for you."

"I'm okay dad. The kids need me. I have to go. I'll call back soon."

"Carol. Wait. Carol." Edgar threw the phone on its base and stormed into the kitchen to find Edith crying.

"What are you crying for? Carol is the one being abused."

Edith's piercing eyes shot daggers at him, and he knew why. He averted eye contact with her. "So you've known about Jacob beating on her and you never told me about it? Why not?" Edgar slammed his hands on the countertops.

Edith wiped her last tear. "What could you say to her, to console her about her husband beating her when she witnessed you do the same to me for so many years?"

"I would've killed him after the first time."

"Why are you so upset? I thought you would be in favor of a man slapping his wife around like you did me."

"Edith..." Edgar lowered his head. "Carol is my daughter. I'm supposed to protect her. I love her so much."

"So you must've hated me then with all the pain you caused me."

"Edith...I have to make things right for Carol." Edgar darted out of the kitchen and back to the phone.

He dialed his son's number. "Hello. Jacob has been beating on your sister. Get over here now."

# *7*

"Dad, I got here as fast as I could. What happened?"

Edith came from the kitchen when she heard her son's voice. They embraced one another.

"Your father is overreacting."

Edgar's eyes widened. "I'm overreacting, but Carol has broken ribs."

Mark's mouth gaped open. "She what?"

Edith cringed.

"Yes. Carol told me that her ribs are broken and that her face is blue and black. So how am I overreacting?" His head was spinning, he sat down in his lazy chair hoping to slow down the rapid beats of his heart.

Edith went to grab him a glass of water. She returned as Edgar was recapping his conversation with Carol to his son.

"…so she's at some friend's house." Edgar rubbed his temples.

"You know she's with Sheila, right?"

"She said she wasn't when I asked her."

"She doesn't have many friends, especially not ones she would trust to share this trauma with."

"Yeah, but we practically raised Sheila too, so I would think that she would have called to tell us that Carol was with her and is alright."

"Dad, you know Carol and Sheila can be tight-lipped about each other when they want to."

"Yeah, you're right."

"Mom." Mark stood up and moved closer to her. "You knew that Jacob had beaten Carol before, and you never told us? Why not?"

Edith saw the disappointment in Mark's eyes. "I, I didn't want Carol to have to deal with both your father and I trying to convince her to stay with him for the sake of the kids."

Edgar interjected, "I wouldn't dare tell Carol to stay with that good for nothing..."

Edith's eyebrows furrowed. "Well, I assumed you would, and as for you, I know how protective you are of your sister. I didn't want you to do something that you would live to regret."

"Mom, I'm confused, why would you want Carol to stay with Jacob if he's been beating on her?"

"Honey, there are just some things you won't understand. There are some things that I don't understand." Edith lowered her head and went to her room.

Mark took a seat on the couch and rubbed his temples. Frustrated, he spoke. "So what do you want to do dad? I've been trying to talk myself out of hurting Jacob. I can't go to jail with a baby on the way, but I can't just let him get away with what he's done to my sister."

"Well, your mother won't like it, but I think that we should go pay Jacob a visit."

Mark agreed.

Edgar grabbed his coat from the coat rack, and the duo went out into the cold winds in search of Jacob.

\*\*\*

They sat outside of Carol and Jacob's house wondering what they would do if Jacob did answer the door.

Edgar was the first to get out of the car. Mark followed.

They banged on the door. No one answered. Mark remembered that he had a spare key to the house and used it. They entered to find the house dark.

They heard whimpering coming from upstairs. Mark flew up the stairs only to find Jacob laying on the floor in the kids room sobbing. Out of breath, Edgar finally made it up to the room.

Mark flicked the light on. "Jacob, why are you crying? You hurt Carol, she didn't hurt you."

Edgar recognized the familiar look of sorrow and contempt on Jacob's face. Memories flooded his senses. He dragged his feet out into the hallway and slumped against the wall.

Jacob came out of his trance and jumped to his feet. Mark mistook Jacob's movement as a threat and the two men wrestled.

"Mark, gon' man. Get off me."

"I bet my sister screamed for you to stop but obviously, you didn't." Mark slammed Jacob to the floor and kicked him hard in his ribs.

Jacob was in pain, but he jumped up to tackle Mark. His attempt failed.

Mark slammed him down to the floor again. He circled Jacob and kicked him repeatedly. "What's wrong, can't handle somebody your size? That's why you had to pick on my sister." Mark kicked Jacob hard again.

Jacob coughed up blood.

"That's enough." Edgar came back in the room and pulled Mark away from Jacob.

Mark pulled away from his dad and hovered over Jacob. He held Jacob's face to stare him in the eyes. "If you ever put your hands on my sister again..." He nudged him in the face with his pointer finger.

What was not said was understood by all in the room.

"I'm sorry. I'm sorry. It won't happen again. I'm sorry." Jacob gripped his body in pain.

Mark and Edgar walked out the room.

\*\*\*

"Pick up the phone. Pick up the phone will ya." Michele continued to let the phone ring.

"Hello."

"Uh, hello. Who is this? Put Jacob on the phone."

"It's me." Jacob winced.

"Are you ok?" Her pitch elevated. Her heart pounded.

"I don't think so. Can you come take me to the hospital?" Jacob ended the call.

"Hospital? Jacob. Jacob." Michele rushed out of the house to Jacob's rescue.

# *8*

"Carol, is everything okay?" Sheila asked.

Carol sat on a stool at the island countertop with her head in her hands. She looked up with her sad eyes at the sound of Sheila's voice. "Everything is just so messed up. I hadn't spoken with my parents all week. My dad called the other day, and I finally decided to tell him what happened. He said he was going to kill Jacob. I don't want my dad to hurt him. Jacob is still the father of my children."

"Hmph. Maybe that's what Jacob needs, a man to show him how it feels to be beat on. And you can always get another dad for the kids."

"Sheila."

"What? I have no sympathy for that man." Sheila pulled the chicken from the refrigerator and laid it on the counter.

"Jacob and I may never be together again, but I still want him to have a relationship with his kids, eventually."

"May? You said you two 'may' never get back together as if you're leaving room for the possibility?" Sheila dropped the cutting knife and braced her hands on the island countertop. "Don't tell me that you're thinking about getting back with Jacob."

"Uh... no. I'm not. I just used the wrong word, I guess."

"Carol, please don't get back with him. If he promised before not to hit you again, but he still did, then you should know you can't trust him. I don't ever want to have to bury you because he beat you to death." Sheila's voice quivered.

"I heard his story about why he started drinking and acting out of character. His actions are inexcusable, but at least now I have an idea of why he was acting the way he was."

"Please don't tell me that his 'woe is me' story is getting to you, is it?"

"No, it's just that you can't automatically turn your feelings off for someone. He hurt me to my core, but as crazy as it may sound, I still love him."

Sheila dropped the knife on the counter once again and rounded the island to look Carol closely in her eyes. She put the back of her hand against Carol's forehead.

Carol smirked as she moved Sheila's hand. "I don't have a fever. I'm not delirious."

"I know that love is a powerful thing, but the love that you have to have for yourself and your safety has to be greater than your love for him, or for any man for that matter." She hugged Carol and went to turn on an eye on the stove to heat a pan.

"I know Sheila. I'm not saying that I want to get back with Jacob or that I will, there are just so many emotions running through me now, love, hate, fear, distrust. And then to top it all off, I've been getting these strange texts from only God knows who."

"Texts? Don't tell me that Jacob is harassing you, because then I'll kill him dead."

"Calm down Sheila. They're not from Jacob. Not sure from who, but I think they're from a woman. She keeps saying that she had him first, and she'll have him again."

"So you mean to tell me that not only was he beating on you, but he was cheating on you?"

"I never got the feeling that he was cheating, but then again, I never thought he would hit me."

"Carol?"

"What?"

"What did the texts say?"

"I had him first and I'll have him again. He's mine. Things along that line."

"Who taunts someone like that, unless they're in high school?" Sheila shrugged her shoulders.

With her head in her hands, Carol rubbed her temples. "Sherlock, I mean Sheila, my head is pounding right now. I don't want to talk about this anymore. I'm going to check on the kids and then take a nap. Wake me when the food is done, please?" Carol left to take a nap in the den.

"Ok and I'll be Sherlock, Matlock, and whatever lock I need to be to get to the bottom of who's sending you those texts if you want me to... Men, you can't trust them."

Sheila thought back to why she really could not trust men. She stepped out onto her patio to smoke a cigarette.

*Sheila. Are you awake? It's me, your Uncle Tommy.* Tommy, her mother's brother, knelt beside her bed and shook her to see if she was awake. She feigned sleep, although that never worked for her the times before. *Ladybug, wake up. You know what Uncle Tommy wants.* He slipped his hand under the covers and began to run his hand along her thighs. She balled herself up tightly. *I knew you weren't sleep Ladybug. I knew you weren't.* He began to tickle her, only she wasn't laughing, she was crying. *Shhh, Ladybug. Don't cry. You don't want your mother to hear us do you? You know she'll be mad at you, and not me, right? Come on, roll over and be a good girl.*

Fearing that her mother would blame her and be mad at her for the things her Uncle Tommy did to her, she had been obliging his lewd requests ever since she was nine years old. She was now twelve. Tommy took off his pants and climbed on top of Sheila. *Ladybug, open them. I wanna make you feel good.* He entered her and began thrusting furiously. Sheila's tears flowed onto her pillow as she wished his convulsions and guttural moans would end soon. Finally, he was done. *Ladybug, you always know what to do to make Uncle Tommy feel good. Now make sure you get up and clean up after yourself. Remember this is our secret.* He leaned down and kissed her cheek as she rolled away from him. *I love you Ladybug.*

She inhaled the last of her cigarette and was brought back to the present day with her cell phone ringing on the kitchen counter.

"Hello beautiful. How are you?" Troy's deep voice serenaded her through the phone.

"I'm fine, and you?" She tried to be as casual as possible, but ever since high school, he always managed to erupt emotions in her that she worked hard to keep dormant.

"I'm good. I just wish you wouldn't push me away like you do. Why can't I see you more often?"

"Troy, how long have you known me?"

"Since high school."

"Well then, you should know by now that I'm the 'no strings attached' type of woman. You act like you're fine with that for a while, but then you have these cycles of asking more of me than you know I'm willing to give."

Troy blew out a loud sigh. "I know. I've tried time and time again to leave you alone."

"Yeah, like when you went AWOL for like three years some years ago," Sheila mumbled under her breath and rolled her eyes.

"What did you say?"

"Oh, nothing." She laughed.

"Alright, smart aleck." He smiled and propped his feet up on the ottoman in front of his loveseat. He loved her smoky voice. "I see what you try not to show.

"Oh yeah, what's that?"

"I see the good in you, I see the beauty in you."

"Well, at least I know you're not blind." Sheila giggled.

"I've always wanted more from you than what you give me in bed. I want your mind, body, and soul."

Sheila shuddered. Chills ran down her spine. "I, um, I, am not going through this with you again. I am who I am." Sheila hated how Troy had the power to make her rethink not giving her heart to a man, but she could not trust them, especially not after that scum Uncle Tommy.

"Okay, Ms. Independent. I want to be with you, and I don't see that changing anytime soon." Troy was frustrated with the speed at which his relationship was maturing with Sheila, which was at a snail's pace, but he knew she was the one for him so he would wait. "Are we still on for tonight? My place or yours?"

Sheila scratched her forehead searching for the words to say. Troy had caught her off guard again with talks of them being together. "Um, about that…"

## *9*

Jacob could not seem to shake Michele ever since he asked her to take him to the hospital that night. She poked and prodded at him until he finally admitted to her at the hospital that Carol had taken the kids and left him, but he never told her exactly why. She stopped by one Tuesday after his counseling session to deal with his anger and drinking to bring him dinner and to discuss the twins as a bridge to see him.

"Hi, Jacob. How are you?"

"I'm fine. Thanks again for getting me the job with my new firm. I owe you."

Michele smirked. He did not know what lengths she went through to get him that job once she found out he had been out of work. She knew exactly how she wanted Jacob to repay her.

"Oh, you're welcome. It was my pleasure helping you out." She bent over in front of him showing her cleavage as she added Thai noodles onto a plate for him.

"And thanks so much for stopping by with dinner tonight. You know, Carol mostly cooked. I know how to make pancakes, you know breakfast foods, but nothing else." Jacob snickered.

"Don't worry about it. I'm here for you whenever and however you need me." Michele winked and cooed.

"Soooo…" Michele sat down next to Jacob with her plate. "It's been a few months since you and Carol have been apart. Do you really think that you two will get back together?"

Jacob dropped noodles on his lap.

"Oh, let me get that for you." Michele reached to grab them, but let her hands roam his inner thigh before scooping the noodles up and discarding them in a napkin.

Jacob cleared his throat. He gulped down his water before he spoke. "Thanks." He made eye contact with her but quickly put his head down noticing the alluring look in her eyes.

"I pray we do."

"Hunh?"

"You asked if I thought that Carol and I will get back together, and I said, I pray that we do."

Michele rolled her eyes. "Oh that's nice, but you know everything happens for a reason. Whatever it is that tore you all apart may have been necessary to show you that you two really don't belong together."

Jacob's face creased all over. He and Carol should be together. She did not deserve what he did to her. "Thanks for everything Michele, but I just remembered that I have some things I need to finish up for work. Talk to you soon."

Michele hated that she even brought up Carol's name. Just the mention of it seemed to be ruining her night with Jacob. "Wait, we still haven't talked about the boys, your sons. Have you told Carol about them yet? About me?" Michele ripped the buttons from a pillow on the loveseat.

Jacob's eyebrows furrowed. He stared at her.

"No, I can't tell Carol about it now, but I won't put off meeting them any longer." Jacob sighed and rubbed his forehead. "How about we meet Saturday at Navy Pier around noon?" Jacob now stood in the front door ready to usher Michele out.

Michele smiled. "Great. I can't wait. I mean I know the boys will be excited to finally meet you. Goodnight Jacob." Michele waved as she walked to her car in the driveway.

He was not hungry anymore. Jacob threw out the remainder of his food. All he wanted to do was to see his wife and kids. He grabbed his phone off the arm of the couch and dialed Carol's number again. She did not answer. It went to her voicemail. "Hello,

Carol? Can you please pick up the phone or at least call me back? It's been months. Far too long. I haven't seen you or the kids. I miss tucking Kaylee and J.J. in at night. I miss waking up to you, and them rushing into our room to turn the TV on for them to watch cartoons on Saturday mornings."

"Please try recording your message again."

He hated that lady's voice. Her voice was the only one he had heard for the past few months when he called Carol's phone. He shook his head thinking about whenever he stopped by, Sheila did not hesitate to run her hand from one side of her throat to the other in a slitting motion when she would catch him sitting outside of her house. He had not spoken with Carol's parents or brother since his fight with Mark. How could he get to Carol to reason with her to at least let him see the kids?

For as much as Jacob dreaded the thoughts racing through his head, he knew what he needed to do next.

***

He rang the doorbell and stepped back.

Edith opened the door and was surprised to see Jacob on her front porch.

"Who is it?" Edgar called out.

Edith's voice was barely audible, "I'm sorry for what they did to you, but I think you should go. Mark is here too."

Edgar made his way to the door. "What the hell are you doing here?" He nudged past Edith.

Mark appeared at the door as well.

"I didn't come here for trouble. I need to talk to you guys. May I, please?" Jacob cast his eyes down.

"We should at least listen to what he has to say." Edith urged her husband and son to step aside. They did so, and Jacob made his way to the living room following Edith.

Edgar and Mark grunted as they entered the living room. They clenched their jaws and balled up their fists tightly. Their nostrils flared. Their hatred for Jacob was apparent.

Jacob hesitated to speak. His shoulders were tight. His feet were flat on the floor. He had to be ready to move at any moment.

Mark stood up with his arms crossed over his chest and his solid legs spread apart comfortably.

Edgar soon sat on the edge of his chair with one fist balled into the other palm, and his elbows braced on his knees. His teeth were clenched. He was full of mixed emotions. He hated that he and Jacob had abusing their wives as common ground. "Ok, so what do you have to say for yourself?"

Jacob was honest and detailed as he recapped the events and news that led to his drinking and the extent of his abuse towards Carol. He constantly noticed how tightly both Edgar and Mark were balling their fists.

Edith sat in torment as she listened to Jacob. In her mind, when Carol described the abuse it was not as bad as she received from Edgar; but for Jacob to detail how he violated her daughter, she hated herself at that moment for encouraging Carol to go back to and stay with Jacob.

"I can't..." Edith shrieked and rushed from the room with her mouth covered as tears streamed down her face.

Mark's mouth tightened. Jacob not only hurt his sister, but now he was upsetting his mother. He knew it must have been hard for her to hear the events, especially since she experienced abuse from his father for much of the early part of their marriage. He edged closer and closer to Jacob with both of his fists balled at his sides.

Jacob stood up, flat-footed ready for whatever Mark may have tried to do to him.

Edgar extended his arm out to prevent his son from getting any closer to Jacob.

"Mark, have a seat."

"I don't want to dad."

"I said, have a seat."

The deep vibrations of Edgar's tone alerted Mark to stay back.

Edith had calmed down. She returned downstairs, unseen, and stood in the entryway of the living room listening to her husband speak.

Edgar fixed dark and pained eyes on Jacob before he spoke. "I know that Carol may have told you of what I did to her mother when we were younger, so you think that you and I have something in common? That I should forgive you? You think that we should move past this? Perhaps you think that I understand you to the point where I will help you get Carol, your family back? Well, if that's what you think, then you have another thing coming." He stood. "Carol is my daughter. My one and only girl. My baby girl. I vowed that I would never stand by and let a man hurt her the way I…" Edgar's eyes misted from flashbacks of the pain he saw in Edith's eyes whenever he would beat her. He shook his head slowly as he looked up to stare at Jacob.

"I can't change the past, but I won't let history repeat itself. So help me God, if it's up to me, you'll never see Carol or the children again. Now get the hell out of my house."

"Dad…Mr. Matthews…can't we try to work this out?"

Edgar stood stoic.

"How would you have felt if Mrs. Matthews kept you away from your kids?" Jacob could feel his ears burning.

Edgar straightened his posture even more. "I said get out." His eyes narrowed in on Jacob as he pointed to the front door.

Mark went over and stood next to his father.

Jacob noted the men's stalwart behavior and headed to the door.

Edith grabbed his arm as he walked past her. "I'll try to work on him and Carol. You deserve to see your kids no matter what."

"Thanks, Ma." He leaned in to kiss her on her cheek but felt Edgar's presence behind him and decided to leave sooner.

Eye to eye, Edith stared at Edgar.

"What?"

"I can't believe you. You beat me senseless the one time I threatened to leave you and take the kids, but you help in keeping Jacob from seeing his?"

"Edith… I, I…" The words just would not come out of him, he hung his head as he walked past Edith headed to his workshop in his garage.

"I'm sorry ma." Mark held his mother tightly.

"Oh sweetie, it's not your sorry I need."

# *10*

"Why won't you just give Troy a real chance?" Sheila snapped her neck hard at Carol.

"I see how you look when you hear his ringtone on your phone. How you glow after you come back home from being with him. You glowed more the night you went on a date with him and didn't have sex than when you do go out and have mind-blowing sex with him, as you say." Carol stuffed her finger in her mouth and pretended to gag.

Sheila stared at Carol. "I don't like you." She laughed.

Carol buckled over in laughter. "Just admit it, you really do like him. He's the only one you've ever given as much time to as you have. The only one you've dated for as long as you have, since high school girl."

"For your information, he and I are not dating. I've just known him longer and periodically see him more often than the other men I fellowship with."

"Oh, so is that what it's called now, fellowship?" Carol laughed even harder.

"That's what I call it." Sheila smirked.

"So since you're not dating him, does he know about the other men that you 'fellowship' with?"

"Um, uh, um, no."

"See. There it is right there. You are so blunt and upfront about how you are with the men that you don't really care for, but for you to hide your other 'fellowships' from Troy obviously means that he's special to you. You don't want him to see you in a certain way."

"And what way is that?"

Carol sat tight-lipped.

"Hmmm…Look mom, I don't need you nagging me about Troy. I like things the way they are between he and I and I plan to keep them that way. Well, at least until I end things with him for good, soon." Sheila became solemn.

"I'm not nagging. I just know that you are a great woman. He's always been a stellar guy and so into you all these years. I remember when he was running down the hall freshman year and ran right into you. He was going so fast that he knocked you to the floor. I just knew that you were going to jump to your feet and check him like how you did everyone else, but I guess he hit the right button for you because you just stared into his light brown eyes. You two stared at each other as he helped you to your feet and picked up your things for you. He's been sweet on you ever since."

Sheila pretended to play an imaginary violin mocking Carol's dramatic retelling of Sheila and Troy's first encounter.

"You've never given him a real chance, you just push him away and send him running somewhere across the country for a while." Carol shook her head. "I want you to stop running away from him, from love. Embrace it."

"Love. Ha. You want me to embrace love? What did 'love' do for you? Left you with broken ribs and a busted face..." Sheila silenced herself seeing Carol tense up.

"I'm sorry Carol. I wasn't trying to offend you. I got caught up in all this talk of love." Sheila reached out to grab Carol's hand.

Carol pulled back from Sheila. "It's okay. Let me go check on the kids." Carol left the room with her head low, gripping her stomach.

"Damn! I sure can put my foot in my mouth sometimes."

*Ooh baby baby, I feel your love surrounding me
Ohh ohh ooh, baby baby, makin' love between
the sheets...*

With a smile in her eyes that she hated to admit, Sheila let the Isley Brothers', "Between the Sheets", ringtone play longer before she answered her phone.

"Hey." She growled trying to sound agitated.

"Hi gorgeous. How are you?"

"I'm fine, except that I just put my foot in my mouth with Carol."

"It'll be alright, you and Carol never stay mad long with each other."

"Yeah, yeah." Sheila laughed. "You're so optimistic, I guess that's why she pushes me to be with you." Sheila covered her mouth. She regretted sharing that with Troy.

Troy chuckled. "That's why I've always liked Carol. She's smart. With me in one ear and her in the other, you and I should be married soon."

"Married? Me? I think not." Sheila stood and paced the floor. Troy had mentioned marriage again.

"Sheila? Sheila? Are you still there?"

Sheila recognized that the phone was down by her side as she paced the floor. She must have missed what he was saying. She put the phone back up to her ear. "Yeah, I'm here. What were you saying?"

"I was saying that I know we've never technically been an official couple, but I've always known that you are the one for me, and I've told you that several times. I think I've shown it too." Troy rubbed his face.

Sheila bit her nails.

"But this is not something that I want to discuss with you over the phone. We can talk about this later during dinner."

"Oh, there's no need to discuss this yet again. You know what I want from you." A sly smile crept across Sheila's face. "Don't make this more than what it is. I say, let's skip dinner tonight and get right down to business." She laughed.

Troy huffed as he spoke. "Sheila, why do you think that I waited so long before we finally had sex?"

"I don't know Troy, you tell me why." She rolled her eyes.

"I knew from the moment that we stared into each other's eyes freshman year that you were different, special. The more I got to know you, the more you proved me right."

"Troy, you know I ain't into all this mushy stuff. Are we hooking up tonight or what?"

"Sheila, you agreed that we would go out for dinner tonight." Troy was getting disconcerted.

"I know, but I've changed my mind, so either I meet you at your house tonight or we not meet at all." Sheila ended the call.

Troy was flustered with only seeing Sheila between the sheets. He wanted more from her than what she offered in the bedroom, which was a lot. She was the best he ever had. He knew it was not because of all the tricks she had up her sleeve in the bedroom, but because of the unspoken connection and chemistry they shared. He wanted to give her more of himself than toe-curling sex, but he knew if he did not agree to let her come to his house that night he might not see her for a while, that pained him.

He was not ready to take that chance.

*Be here by 9.* Troy pressed send.

\*\*\*

Carol was glad that Sheila finally left the house. The kids were asleep, and she no longer had to muffle her sounds of throwing up. She could not help but to reflect on what could have possibly made her sick for the past couple of months. She went out on the patio to take in the night stars. They shined so brightly in contrast to the darkness in her life. *What am I going to do? Divorce Jacob? Go back to teaching to support myself and the kids? So much to decide in what seems like so little time. Mr. Simpson has been calling me incessantly asking if I will teach the Early Learners summer program, but I haven't answered him yet. Maybe I should. Then I can move out and get my own apartment and give Sheila back her personal space. It's only been a few months since I left him, but I guess it's time that I move on and start a new chapter in my life.*

Carol was headed down a line of more questions to herself, but she felt the urgency to rush to the bathroom to relieve herself of what she had for dinner. She washed her face and gargled. She headed to the kids' room to make sure they were sound asleep. She grabbed her laptop and headed back out to the deck.

*Dear Mr. Simpson,*

*I appreciate you extending the invitation for me to teach the Early Learner's program this summer. You know that working with primary students is my passion. I have missed being around them and helping to shape their future, so yes I will teach the program. I have also heavily considered returning back to my position as a teacher in the fall, and I agree to that as well. Thank you for keeping me in mind, and I look forward to getting back to work within the next couple of weeks.*

*Sincerely,*
*Carol Rodgers*

Carol proofread the message and said a quick prayer to make sure that she was making the right decision. She pressed send.

\*\*\*

Troy collapsed on top of Sheila. His breathing was uneven, and she was struggling to return hers to its normal pace. He placed tender kisses on her neck and softly traced her thighs with his fingers, but she pushed him off of her.

Troy exhaled loudly. "Why did you push me off of you like that?"

"I told you no romance, just sex." Sheila swiveled in the bed until she was upright, and her legs dangled off the sides of the bed. She reached for a cigarette and lit it, she got one pull before Troy snatched the cigarette from her mouth mid puff and left to throw it in the toilet.

"I hate it when you smoke. You're too beautiful for that." His sun-kissed skin caressed Sheila's face as he stood in front of her.

She melted at his touch, but quickly reminded herself that she could not trust men, even though Troy had been a constant over the years.

"I have to go." Sheila searched for her panties.

"Why? Spend the night with me."

"Why? You know why. Why won't you just let things be between us the way they have been? Why do you have to go and get all sentimental on me? I just want to have sex. Unadulterated, no strings attached sex." She scratched her forehead. Her eyes shifted rapidly from side to side. "I think that we have gotten too comfortable with one another. Let's make tonight the last time we see each other." Sheila cleared the lump in her throat. She located her bra and put it on, then slipped into her dress.

Troy was silent. He inched closer and closer to Sheila.

His presence was magnetic. She stood still.

He stood in front of her, cupped her chin, and pecked at her lips until she allowed his tongue to enter her mouth. The balcony doors were open, and the early summer breeze grazed her skin as he kissed her. Deeply. She relaxed in his arms as he firmly planted one hand on the small of her back and the other around her neck willing her head the way he wanted to as he kissed her passionately.

Her resolve was fading, but flashbacks of her Uncle Tommy made her push Troy off of her.

"Sheila, don't go." He reached out to her.

"I can't stay, I have to go." Sheila grabbed her purse and raced to the elevator. She fought hard to keep the tears from escaping her eyes. She made it to the front door of the downtown high-rise and handed the valet her ticket.

"Ma'am, are you okay?" The observant young man spoke in concern.

Sheila brushed at the tears that evaded her face and stood up straighter. "Yes. Can you just hurry to get my car?"

He nodded and rushed off to get her car.

Sheila barely allowed him to get out of the car before she slid in the seat, put her foot on the brake, shifted the gear into drive, closed the door, and sped off, in what all seemed like simultaneous movements. She drove for quite some time before her tears clouded her vision. She pulled over to the shoulder of the expressway. She inhaled and exhaled loudly before her breaths became too short to stomach. She let out a long piercing wail. "I hate you Uncle Tommy. I hate you for what you did to me all those years. I hate you momma. I hate you for not noticing and stopping the torment that I was going through. I hate you both…" Sheila let out another guttural wail before she collapsed in sobs over the steering wheel.

Although the drive from downtown Chicago to Sheila's suburb was forty-five minutes without traffic, it took her almost two hours to get home given her emotional breakdown along the way. Troy had called and texted her several times since she left him, but she would not dare answer his calls or reply to his texts.

She wiped her face and tried to remove any trace of her crying just in case she ran into Carol in the house. She was too exhausted to answer any questions. She entered the house completely drained and distraught. She did not even hear Carol vomiting in the bathroom as she retreated to her bedroom.

# *11*

Jacob was getting to know the twins, but Michele was making it difficult for him to spend quality time with them because she was always there, hogging the boys time with him. He hung out with them at her brother's house hoping Michael or Michael's wife, Rita, could keep Michele occupied while he got to know the boys better.

"So Jacob, how does it feel man? How does it feel to have twin sons, this old?" Michael rustled Jacob Jr.'s hair as they sat around the table eating burgers and chips in the backyard one Saturday morning after tossing around the football.

"Jacob, you okay? Is there anything else you need?" Michele winked at him from the kitchen door.

"I'm fine. Thanks."

"Yes, you are," Michele mumbled.

"See, you shouldn't have flirted with her when we were younger. You haven't been able to shake her since." Michael laughed and took a sip of his beer. "Twins, why don't you two go into the den and play the game. I want to talk to your dad."

The boys left. The men were silent for a minute.

Jacob broke the silence. "Mike?" Jacob's face furrowed. He put distance between himself and Michael.

"Yeah?" Michael knew exactly where the conversation was going.

"I thought we were boys man. I thought you had my back?"

"Jacob…."

"Man, why you didn't tell me that I had sons? Eleven-year-old twin sons that I wasn't there to raise." Jacob shook his head.

"Mike?" Jacob tried getting Michael's attention.

"Jake, we *are* boys. You're like my brother."

"I can't tell!"

"I've been stuck in the middle all this time. I'm sorry man. You're my boy, she's my sister, my blood for God's sake! I tried to get her to tell you about them so many times over the years because I knew they needed you, and you would've wanted to know about them, but man that wasn't my decision to make."

"Eleven years and nobody tells me anything." Jacob crushed the can he was holding with a lone hand.

Mike stepped back.

"I just don't get it. Michele said she wanted me to pursue my dream of playing football with nothing stopping me, but man that ain't right. And then for all of y'all to go along with her secret and not tell me, this is some bull-"

"Jake, I'm sorry man. We're all sorry. My parents were upset that she got pregnant at such a young age-"

"But that should've been the very reason they wanted me to know so that I could be a father to my kids."

"Yeah, I hear ya man, but you know there's always been something different about Michele."

Jacob laughed thinking about how *different* and intense Michele could be.

"Seriously man. Like when she likes or loves something, she really obsesses over it, to the point where it can be scary."

Jacob's eyebrows raised.

"She's my sister, so I couldn't flat out tell you not to mess with her then. I tried to tell you on the low, but you didn't seem to catch my hints."

Jacob sat back in his chair and rubbed his chin.

"She can be scary at times."

Jacob sat up. "What do you mean?"

Michael let out a slow deep breath that shifted the mood. "You know we didn't move here until junior high right."

"Yeah."

"Well, before we got settled here we moved around quite a bit because Michele always managed to get kicked out of the schools she was in because of a boy."

"What?" Jacob's eyes widened. He was stunned learning that fact about Michele that had been hidden from him all of these years.

"She's smart. She used to obsess over her grades when she was younger, but when she hit puberty, her obsession changed to boys. We had to move three times within two years because she would crush on a boy, find out about the other girls who liked him and things would go downhill from there."

"What do you mean?"

"She threatened them to stay away from the boy she liked at that time and if the girls didn't take heed to what she said, she followed through with her threats."

Jacob's forehead creased.

"At first she did little things to the girls like putting red liquid in a seat to make a girl look like she had her period and bled all over herself. Then she would to spread hurtful rumors about the girls being promiscuous."

Jacob shook his head in disbelief.

"Yeah, man. At first, no one could prove she was doing those things, but after so many incidences throughout the year, everything pointed back to her, so we moved on to the next school to start fresh. She would get a new crush, and her terror would start all over again. She does whatever she feels is necessary to get what she wants." Michael shook his head. "With each school, she became more and more bold. She started cutting girl's hair and then she just escalated to fighting them until our parents moved us on to the next school, the next city."

Jacob stood up. His eyes were wide. "Man, why didn't you ever tell me any of this? Why wasn't she put in juvie for any of that stuff?" Jacob wrung his hands together.

"My parents put her in therapy and the therapist managed to smooth things over with the courts. She was diagnosed as having Histrionic Personality Disorder and Bipolar Disorder. The therapy seemed to work after the last incident she had during junior high. She seemed normal again once we moved here, not obsessing and lashing out over stuff, especially boys."

Jacob stood still rubbing his forehead trying to make sense of what he was told. "Histri who?"

"Histrionic."

"What's that?"

"It's like she has to control her partner through emotional manipulation or seduction on one hand, but then on the other, she has a weird dependency on them. She feels like she has to be at the center of attention for them…Look J, I know you want to know why I never told you any of this stuff, but like I said she's my sister. You and I are close, always have been, but my loyalty lies with my sister first. Do you understand?"

Jacob let out a loud sigh. "Yeah, I get it."

Michael exhaled and smiled. "So how are you really doing? I know finding out about the twins was a lot on you, but to lose your job and your wife and kids. Man, that's crazy." Michael took a sip of beer he was nursing. "You've never told me why she left you man, what's up with that?"

Jacob paced the floor.

"What's up J?" Michael walked over to Jacob. He spoke low. "Did you cheat on her? Was it with Michele? You can tell me man, I won't judge you."

Jacob began pacing the deck a bit before he spoke. "No, I didn't cheat on Carol." His hands sweated. He wondered if he should tell Michael exactly why Carol left him. "I don't want to go into why she left me right now, just know that I am not the same man that she left. I've been going to counseling trying to understand who I am and how to better control...If only she would let me show her that." Jacob sat back down and rubbed his face slowly. "As for the twins, of course, I was shocked to find out that I had kids other than the ones I saw come into this world. It bothers me a lot to know that I missed out on so much of their lives, but I won't miss another moment of them. I'll fight hard to make sure that all of my kids get to know one another."

Michael saw the angst on Jacob's face and patted his back before he went back to his seat.

"How are you going to make that happen, Carol won't even let you see the kids?"

"I don't know, but I'll figure it out."

"I know my sister, and as I just told you, she can be a handful. You say you didn't cheat with her to make Carol leave, but what exactly is going on between you and my sister? Since she's come back into town, it's been Jacob this and Jacob that. You haven't led her on, have you?" Michael sat up straight and focused his attention on Jacob.

"Her disorder must have kicked back into gear or something." Jacob laughed.

"Seriously bro, you sure you aren't leading her on in the least bit?"

"I swear I'm not man." Jacob jumped out of his seat. He would not take another beat down from anyone else's brother. "I swear I'm not man. It started out with her just contacting me about the boys, but since I've been spending more time with them, she's starting to make 'us' comments. You know what's so ironic?" Jacob did not let Michael answer. "The twin's birthday is the same day as my little Jacob Jr." Jacob laughed. "I have two Jacob Jr.'s. What's even funnier than that is to add insult to injury, Michele suggested that we have a party for the twins and little J.J. together. I can't even get Carol to talk to me or let me see the kids, so how can I get her to have a joint birthday for my sons starring two Jacob Jr.'s?"

Although Jacob was hurting on the inside, he could not help but to laugh at the thought of Carol actually agreeing to the party.

"Man, I'm not even thinking about being with another woman other than Carol. I want my family back." Jacob steadied his hands on the deck rails as he let the rays of the sun embrace him. He closed his eyes rather than let the tears fall from them.

***

Jacob sat alone in his living room reminiscing on the time he had been spending with his twins. He had to admit that Michele and her aunt did a great job with them. They were very respectful, honor roll students, athletic, and humorous. He developed a soft spot for them. He could not come to terms with calling the oldest twin Jacob Jr., so he nicknamed him Coby, his abbreviation of the name 'Jacob'.

His thoughts left the twins and settled on his younger children and wife. He missed them terribly. He picked up his phone and dialed Carol's number.

"The number you are calling is no longer in service."

Jacob knew that he was wrong for hitting Carol, but for her to leave, take the kids, and deny him the right to see them or talk to them was too much for him to handle. He resolved that he would go to Sheila's house in the morning and demand that he and Carol come to some amicable agreement regarding seeing his kids. He would try to win her love and trust back in time as well.

He thumbed through reports from work making sure that the bottom lines for each account matched the transactions made over the month. He did that for a while before deciding to surf the channels for something interesting to watch. He lingered on FOX 32 breaking news.

*This just in. There has been a fatal accident at an intersection in Edgebrook. Bystanders say the light was green for the direction that the sedan was traveling in, but the police car sped through going across the traffic and the driver slammed right into the side of the police car, before it spun and then crashed into a light post. The police officers did not sustain any injuries, but the EMT's have reported that the driver of the sedan is in critical condition. Stay tuned for the 9 o'clock news for updates.*

"Wow. I pray for that man and his family." Jacob shook his head and spoke before switching the channel to an action movie. He did not want to hear any more bad news.

Jacob looked down at his phone a third of the way into the movie and noticed that he had ten missed calls from Michele. He saw that she left six voicemails, so hopefully the voicemails would fill him in on what she wanted, and he would not have to call her back. He pressed the voicemail button and put in his code when prompted. He only heard sobs for the first thirty seconds. Then a muffled tear-filled voice spoke. *"Jacob....I'm, we're at the hospital. It's Michael. He was in an accident...Oh God Noooooo."*

The message ended. Jacob was not sure that he heard the message correctly, so he decided to listen to the next message. He turned the sound off on the TV.

*"Ohhhhhhh, no God, Nooooo....Jacob, it's Michael. He's gone. Come to the..."*

The message ended without him knowing exactly where Michele wanted him to go. He was confused. *What does she mean Michael is gone? He didn't say he was going out of town, but wait she said on the first message that she was at the hospital and that he was in an accident. She can't be saying...*

Jacob turned the TV off entirely this time before he listened to the third message Michele left.

Her voice was more audible even though he could tell she was still crying profusely. *"Jacob. It's me. I don't know if you've gotten my other messages, but the boys need you. I need you. Please come as soon as you can. We're at Northwest Community Hospital...Michael. He's gone."* Michele screamed her last words in terror.

She hoped no one would ever know the depth of her anguish.

Jacob was not ready to come to grips with what he thought Michele was saying via her messages. He decided to go to the hospital and find out exactly what was going on.

\*\*\*

"Hello. How are you this evening?" Jacob asked the hospital receptionist.

"I'm doing fine. How are you?"

"Not sure just yet. Do you have a Michael Robinson listed as a patient?"

"You know that visiting hours are over?" She stared at him over her thick-lensed glasses and puckered her lips. "But I can at least check to see if he is a patient here."

Jacob's phone rang. It was Michele.

"What's going on? I'm here at the hospital waiting for the receptionist to tell me what room Michael is in."

"Jacob. He's not in a room." Michele tried to even her breathing. "He died before he made it to the hospital. They took his body down to the morgue already." Michele wept.

Jacob stood frozen in disbelief.

"Jacob, are you there?"

"Uh, yeah. Where are you?"

"We're all in the emergency waiting room."

"I'm heading over there now." Jacob hung up the phone. "Excuse me miss, how do I get to the emergency room?"

"Take this hallway all the way to the end, make a left, and go through the double doors. Take care."

Michele rushed to Jacob the minute she saw him come through the doors. She leaned into his chest and sobbed.

After realizing she would not stop crying on him anytime soon, he embraced her. He managed to escort her to an empty seat next to her mother, but Michele would not let him go, so he sat down next to her.

Everyone seemed to be frozen in time from the news of Michael's sudden death.

"I know this is hard for all of us, but there is nothing more we can do here. The coroner promised to notify us once she determines the exact cause of his death." Michael's father spoke.

Michael's wife let out a gut-wrenching wail.

Michael Sr. gathered his daughter-in-law from the floor and put his arm around her to help her to the car.

Michael's mom spoke. "Come on Michele, get the kids. I'm pretty sure the twins will be a big help with helping to comfort their younger cousins."

"Jacob, I don't want to be alone tonight." Michele looked into his eyes.

"You won't be, you'll be with your family," Jacob whispered to Michele.

"You're my family too. I want to be with you tonight. I don't think that I can make it being around everyone else crying in that house all night."

"Okay. I can stay over there at your parent's house with you."

"No. I don't want to be there tonight, too many memories. Can I stay at your house?"

"Well, what about the boys? They need you."

"I need you too. They'll be alright with my parents and their cousins. Please, Jacob."

Jacob saw the plea in Michele's eyes. "Ok, just for tonight."

Michele squeezed his hand in gratitude. "Mom, you go ahead to the car with the kids, I'm going to ride with Jacob." She smirked.

***

Jacob made it home. He opened the car door for Michele and let her into the house. "There is a bathroom next to the bedroom upstairs at the end of the hall. You can go up and shower there if you like. Try to get some rest."

Jacob dropped down on the couch. The news of Michael's sudden death, one of his oldest and closest friends, was a lot for him to take in so suddenly.

Michele ignored Jacob's suggestion to rest upstairs, but instead sat near him on the couch.

They sat in silence for what seemed like hours before Michele rested her head on Jacob's shoulder. He could tell that she was crying because his shirt was wet where she lay her head. She sniffled. Her chest heaved up and down rapidly. She moved closer to Jacob.

He raised his arm and put it around her shoulder and pulled her in closer to comfort her.

Michele loved her closeness to Jacob. She draped her arm across his stomach and inched even closer to him. For a second, she buried her face in the crook of his arm and inhaled as much as she could of the scent that belonged to only him.

Jacob did not think much of Michele's arm across his stomach. He hated to admit that he enjoyed her being next to him. It had been months since he had been intimate with Carol. He rubbed her arm and leaned down to inhale the sweet apple scent of her hair.

Michele felt his hand caress her arm. She did not want him to stop. She tilted her face to his neck and breathed deep, hoping that the heat of her breath would scintillate him.

His manhood rose. He pulled back some, not wanting to cross the line with her. *I can't get Carol back like this.*

She closed the new distance between them again and began to kiss his neck. She let her hand roam to the bulge in his pants and massaged it.

Jacob moaned. He turned to her. They stared into each other's eyes. Jacob noticed the mixture of pain and longing in Michele's almond shaped eyes. Her smooth pecan skin was so soft. Her plump breasts peeked at him from the top of her blouse.

Michele soaked in every ounce of Jacob's facial features; from his goatee to his square jawline to his hazel-brown eyes. She wanted him, and she knew she would have him that night.

He lowered his head. "Michele, we can't. I'm still married. I love my wife." He was torn. He too was grieving for Michael and wanted to be comforted at that moment. He wanted to feel the warmth of a woman, but she was not his wife.

Michele continued to massage his manhood with one hand and traced circles along his jawline with the other. She whispered in a sultry voice to him, "Jacob, Carol's not here. She hasn't been here for months. You need this." Michele lifted the bottom of her dress and draped one leg over Jacob's and led his hand up her thigh to her panties.

Jacob could not believe where his hand was; a place he had not been in a long time. Michele expertly rubbed the bulge in his pants diluting his senses. He found his hand inside of her, exploring the moistness of her femininity.

Michele pulled Jacob's face closer to her and kissed him feverishly. The deeper the kiss, the deeper his fingers went inside of her. She arched her back. Jacob became more excited and pulled Michele on top of him. He cupped her cheeks as they explored each other's mouths. Michele unzipped Jacob's pants and freed his throbbing penis. She skillfully gripped it as she fell to her knees. Jacob moaned loudly.

Jacob's eyes bulged as she fell to her knees with his shaft still in her hand. Feeling a tinge of guilt, he attempted to stop her, but she put the tip in her mouth, rendering Jacob weak. She licked it like an ice cream cone. With every lick and pull, his shoulders slumped more and more, and his eyes rolled further and further to the back of his head. He was speechless.

Michele figured pleasing Jacob with her mouth was only the beginning for them. She felt the pressure of his hands on her head and his legs stiffen before they relaxed. She knew he was pleased with her work. She wiped her mouth and crawled back up to him until her naked bottom spread across his waist. She had managed to skillfully take her panties off while pleasuring him with her mouth without interrupting the flow. She kissed his neck and lowered his hands to her butt. He gripped each cheek as if his life depended on it. She reached down and fondled his manhood until it was fully engorged again. She lowered herself onto it.

Jacob held her at her waist to prevent her from going further. "Michele, we can't. I don't have on protection." Jacob was trying to come to his senses.

"Don't worry. I'm on the pill." She kissed him senselessly and lowered herself completely onto him.

He moaned. He shook.

Michele wound her hips sensationally as she rode him. The tighter he gripped her butt, the longer he sucked her nipples. She knew she was giving Jacob exactly what he wanted. What he needed.

They climaxed at the same time, and Michele collapsed onto Jacob's chest.

Jacob's head was spinning. "Michele. I'm sorry. I'm sorry for taking advantage of you tonight."

"You didn't take advantage of me. We both needed this. This was bound to happen." She played with his ears. She remembered how much that used to excite him. She licked her lips, then his, over and over and over and over.

Her plan had her right where she wanted to be, but her brother's fate had not turned out the way she wanted it to.

# *12*

It was her first day of the Early Learner's Program and Carol could not stop snacking on everything in sight. She found it odd that the week before she could not manage to keep any food down, but now she seemed hungry every second of the day. She had breakfast filled with pancakes, eggs, turkey bacon, oatmeal, fruit and orange juice, so she could not fathom why it was barely noon and her stomach was growling as if she had not eaten in days.

Carol clapped her hands once and a few children clapped once. She clapped twice. More children followed suit and clapped twice. She clapped three times. All of the students clapped three times. She smiled at them. "Now that I have all you all's attention, I need you to put away your art supplies so that we can prepare for lunch and the physical activity portion for the remainder of your time here."

The kids rushed to clean their areas knowing that she always had a treat for them if they moved swiftly and quietly.

Once all of the kids were seated quietly at their tables with their hands folded, she signaled for the lunch attendant at the door to take them out. They pushed in their chairs as each table was called knowing they would not be returning to Mrs. Rodgers for the day. Carol passed the attendant the bag of goodies as the last student exited the class. She tidied up the room and reviewed her lessons for the following day.

"Carol?"

She jumped. The papers in her hand fell to the floor. She did not know someone else was in the room with her.

"Sorry to startle you." Her coworker Eric rushed over and kneeled to help her gather up the papers.

"No, it's okay. I was just lost in thought, as usual."

"Here." He handed her the last piece of paper he picked up. "Welcome back." He looked directly into her eyes. His gaze was hypnotic. "How are you doing?"

"Uh, uh, thanks. I'm doing good. I just have to get used to being back in a classroom after having been out of one for a few years." She averted further eye contact with Mr. Martinez and continued to tidy up her desk.

"Mr. Simpson says that you will be returning in the fall as well?" He walked up to the side of her trying to engage her face to face.

"Yes. I have to." Carol quickly resented blurting out her last statement. She turned so that her back was to him again.

"You have to?" The pitch in his voice elevated.

Carol realized it was immature and awkward of her to talk to him with her back to him. He was always easy to talk to, she resolved that moment would not be any different. She turned around and noticed his broad shoulders as he stood in front of her with his arms crossed at his chest. She scanned his body and noticed his bow legs, which made him so much more appealing at that moment. His olive toned skin, and curly jet black hair rounded out his sex appeal. Carol fanned herself. *What is wrong with me? Why is Mr. Martinez so attractive right now? I am a married woman.* She could see that he was waiting for a response to his question. "That came out wrong. I was just saying that it's time for me to get back to work. Get back to doing what I love."

Eric could tell that there was something Carol was not sharing with him. "I see you're getting ready to leave, so am I. Can I walk you to your car?"

"Oh sure." Carol smiled at him as she grabbed her bags.

"Cool. We just have to stop by my room so that I can grab my briefcase."

After leaving his room, they made small talk as they walked to the main office to clock out then they headed to Carol's car.

"It's such a beautiful summer day. What do you have planned for the rest of the day?"

"Not much. I'm hungry, so I'll stop by a restaurant and grab something before I get back to Sheila's house and play with the kids in her backyard for a while." Carol tossed her bags in the back of her SUV.

"I remember Sheila. She's your best friend right?"

"Yeah."

"Oh, so she's babysitting the kids for you while you're at work?"

"Not quite," Carol's grin was twofold; she could tell that Eric was fishing for more information about her life, and that was kind of cute to her, but she also grinned thinking on how her babysitter was the complete opposite of Sheila. She hired Jillian, a college student who was home for the summer, to watch Kaylee and J.J. for the four hours a day she worked the summer program.

"I'm sorry if I'm asking too many personal questions. I just miss chatting with you as often as we did before you left."

Carol smiled. "Yeah, we did use to have some great talks."

"Enough questions about me. What about you, are you still with Maria?"

Eric turned his head and squinted his face as if he was trying to get the sun out of his eyes. "Uh, no, we ended over a year ago."

"It's been that long since we've spoken?" Carol was ashamed that she did not keep in better contact with her colleague. She raised one eyebrow. "Involved with someone else then?"

"Actually, you and I haven't talked since you left on your maternity leave before having your son." Eric shoved his hands in his pockets and rocked from his heels to his toes. "And no, I'm not seeing anyone now."

"Aw come on, a great guy like you?" Carol playfully hit Eric on his shoulder.

"I guess I just haven't met the right one yet." He looked down and continued to rock back and forth on his feet.

An awkward silence fell on them.

"Well, I have to go and relieve my babysitter. It was good catching up with you. See you tomorrow."

Carol walked around to the driver's side of her vehicle.

Eric followed her. "You still like sausage McMuffins from McDonalds?" Eric laughed.

Carol laughed. She felt her stomach growl too. "Yes, more now than ever." She rubbed her bloated stomach.

"I'll make sure to bring you one tomorrow."

"Oh, you don't have to go through the trouble."

"No trouble at all. It would be my pleasure. Enjoy the rest of your day."

Eric closed Carol's car door and stood there until she drove out of the parking lot.

\*\*\*

"Mommy, mommy, mommy." Kaylee and J.J. both ran to Carol and held on to her legs.

She leaned down to kiss each of them on top of their heads. "Did you all have a great day today?"

J.J. nodded his head up and down then headed back to play on the swing set Sheila had built in her backyard for the kids.

"Yes, mommy. We had lots of fun with Jillian. We said the alphabet, we said our numbers and we matched our colors. She made up millions of games for us to play out here."

Carol smoothed down Kaylee's ponytails.

"Mommy, I really miss daddy. Like this much." Kaylee stretched out her arms as far apart as she could.

Carol stooped low to talk to Kaylee eye to eye. She hugged her first before speaking to her. "I know you do, sweetie. I'm pretty sure he misses you and J.J. too." Carol paused, "you'll see him soon."

"When?"

Carol's mouth twisted in angst. "Maybe you can see him Saturday."

Kaylee began to jump up and down screaming in a sing-song voice, "I'll see my daddy soon, I'll see my daddy soon."

Carol immediately regretted lying to Kaylee. It was bad enough she would have to see him at Michael's funeral on Saturday, but she was definitely not ready to let him see the kids. She would go and pay her respects and leave before the service began. She tried hard not to think about Jacob, what he did, and what she would have to do where he was concerned. She was not ready to face him on Saturday. *Saturday. Michael's funeral. I don't think I can go Saturday. But he was a great friend to Jacob and I. Okay, maybe seeing Jacob that day will give me with the closure that I need.*

Carol's thoughts were interrupted by Jillian. "Ok, Mrs. Rodgers the kids were great today as usual. See you tomorrow."

*Mrs. Rodgers. If I get divorced, will I keep my married name or go back to my maiden name? I don't want my kids to have a different last name than me.* "Ok Jillian. Thanks so much. See you tomorrow."

Carol's mind was flooded with so many "what if" questions and scenarios. She grew tired all of a sudden. She sat down on a swinging bench where she could have the perfect view of the kids playing in the sandlot while she devoured her Thai Chicken Panini from Panera Bread. She let the kids play for about another hour before she took them in the house to bathe them and put them down for a nap.

She decided to start on dinner while they were asleep.

\*\*\*

"Carol, what is that you're cooking? It smells delish," Sheila inquired as she reached into the refrigerator to grab a bottled water.

"Oh nothing much, just Caesar salad, shrimp fettuccine alfredo, cheesy garlic bread, sautéed vegetables, and Thai chicken. Oh, and to top it off, strawberry cheesecake, chocolate brownies, and vanilla bean ice cream for dessert." Carol nibbled on a piece of the garlic bread.

Sheila's eyebrows furrowed, "Soooo, who else is coming to dinner?"

"No one else. Just you, me, and the kids."

"All that food for us four?"

"Yes." Carol wondered why Sheila found it hard to believe that it would only be the four of them for dinner.

"I guess. Well, you and I can take the leftovers to lunch tomorrow." Sheila sat on a stool at the island; elbows propped up with her head in her hands just staring at Carol. She watched Carol nibble on one thing after another.

"Can you wake the kids for me while I set the table?"

"Sure." Sheila nodded her head up and down slowly baffled by how much Carol seemed to have consumed in the little amount of time she sat at the island staring at her. She looked at her phone. She ignored another call from Troy.

"Mommy, what's for dinner?" Kaylee came into the kitchen rubbing her eyes but smiling.

"Have a seat and you'll see."

Carol fixed the children's plates, and they all began to eat.

"Carol, I think you might want to slow down."

"Hunh?" Carol stuffed more fettuccine into her mouth.

"No offense, but…" Sheila paused to think of exactly how she should phrase her words. "You have packed on a few pounds around your waist and thighs in what seems like just this past week. I mean for a couple of months I was worried because you were getting so thin. I figured it was the stress of what you are going through, but now you're getting thick. Not that that's bad. Just watch it though, emotional eating can have bad effects on your health." Sheila hoped she did not offend Carol.

Carol shook her head. "I don't know how to explain it. I couldn't seem to keep any food down the first few months since I left…but like you said, in this past week I just can't stop eating. My stomach is constantly growling and begging me to eat something." She put a forkful of cheesecake into her mouth.

"Do you think it's something that you need to see a doctor about? Maybe it's a bug."

"I don't think so. Maybe it's just my body's way of coping with the stress of what I've been going through." Carol took a big gulp of apple juice. She began to laugh uncontrollably realizing just how much food she had eaten within the amount of time Sheila had been home.

Carol's laughter was infectious, Sheila laughed too.

"What are you laughing at?" Sheila asked.

"I guess I have eaten enough for a whole village today." She cupped her mouth to keep the food from falling out as she continued laughing. "Kind of like when I was pregnant with Kaylee." Carol wiped her tears of laughter and bit into a brownie.

Sheila sat silently.

"What?"

"Kaylee, J.J., why don't you all go into the den and watch TV. Your mom and I will be in there in a second."

"Okay, Auntie Sheila. Come on, let's go J.J." They left the table and skipped hand in hand to the den.

"Why are you looking like that Sheila?" Carol cleaned the table.

"Carol, you were very nauseous during your first trimester with Kaylee. Everything sent you running to the bathroom, or to the nearest garbage can to empty your stomach and then within a week's time you began to eat everything in sight. I remember because you always had Jacob bring you food from at least two different restaurants for lunch." Sheila tilted her head as her eyebrows raised. "Honey, are you sure you're not pregnant?"

Carol dropped the plates she had in her hand. Fettuccine splattered in one direction while strawberry sauce flew in another. She stared intently at Sheila. "Pregnant? Me pregnant? I can't be Sheila.

Jacob and I have been separated for about four months. How could four months pass and I not know that I'm pregnant?"

Sheila stood. She went to comfort her friend who now had tears streaming down her face, and her hands shook effortlessly. "It's okay Carol. It's okay sweetie." Sheila pulled Carol into her arms. "You've been under so much stress during these past four months that you haven't paid real attention to your body. When was the last time you had your period?"

Carol pulled back from Sheila. She took deep breaths as she wiped the tears from her face. "I don't know."

"Do you chart it in a calendar or anything like that?

"Yeah. Let me check my phone." Carol rushed off to get her phone while Sheila cleaned the floor.

Sheila was just about done cleaning the kitchen when Carol returned. "What took you so long? Couldn't find your phone?" Sheila put the leftovers in the refrigerator. She turned to see why Carol was not responding.

Carol stood in disbelief with her phone in her hand. She saw Sheila's lips moving, but she could not concentrate on what Sheila was saying. She could not get past the last noted date in her calendar.

"What is it honey?" Sheila came from around the island to be closer to Carol. "Was it this month? Last month?

Carol held up her phone to Sheila.

"February 12$^{th}$ was the first day of your last period? So, that means if you are pregnant, you're four months."

"I can't be though. I can't be pregnant, and my husband and I are separated, probably about to get a divorce. What would I do with another baby to take care of by myself?"

"Raise him or her the way you have with Kaylee and J.J. You stayed at home and nurtured them while Jacob was at work and even when he came home you still did the most. Please don't forget that you have me. You have your brother and his wife. You have your parents."

"I'm not sure about my parents. My mom will probably let Jacob see the kids if I were to let the kids be with them sometimes."

"Carol, how long are you going to stay away from your parents and keep the kids away from them? I'm pretty sure you miss them. You all have always been so close and you know they miss their grands."

"Until I'm convinced that they, especially my mom, will respect my wish to not let Jacob see them." Carol shook her head. "But I can't deal with that right now. What if I'm really pregnant?" Carol's eyes widened.

"Before we get into any more hypotheticals, let's see if you actually are pregnant. Come on follow me."

"Where to, the store?"

"No, my bathroom."

"You have a pregnancy kit on standby?"

"In my line of 'work' I have to." Sheila laughed.

"In your line of work? But you're a media relations manager at a hospital, why would you need a pregnancy test for that?" Carol scratched her forehead.

"Not my daytime work, for the 'work' I put in at night, if you know what I mean." Sheila winked and snickered.

Carol smirked and shook her head from side to side. She swatted Sheila's hand.

They went past the den to check in on the kids and then headed upstairs to Sheila's master bath.

Sheila ripped the stick from the box. "Here. Go pee on it, and hurry."

# *13*

Jacob only had a physical attachment to Michele since the night her brother Michael died.

He would have preferred for her to leave after they had sex last night, but she insisted that she spend yet another night with him. The more he suggested that she not stay, the more she did that thing with her tongue that weakened his resolve, thus how he lie there at 5:45 in the morning staring at her naked body shielded only by a bed sheet.

"Michele. Michele. Don't you think you ought to go to your parents' house and be with your mom, your dad, the boys, Michael's wife?"

She moaned and stretched. "Nope."

"I think that you should. You need to be with them now, especially considering the fact that it's the day before the funeral. I'm pretty sure they need your help with some things."

Michele rolled over to kiss Jacob on his lips, but he turned his head and she caught his jaw. "I'm right where I want to be." She nestled closer to him. "Besides, I go there during the day while you are at work and help out as needed. It's not like we are preparing for a BBQ or family reunion, we're saying goodbye to my brother. We're burying Michael." Her stomach churned. Her lips quivered. She dropped her head to his chest. Tears flooded her face.

Out of pity, he rubbed her back.

"I just wish we didn't have to." She jumped from the bed and ran hysterically in tears to the bathroom.

Jacob got up from his bed and put his boxers on. He stepped into his slippers and headed towards the bathroom. As he was turning the knob to enter, Michele was pulling on the door from her side to exit. They collided into one another. Jacob extended his arms to keep Michele from falling, but she accepted them as an invitation to be closer to him. She elevated on her tip toes.

"Michele." He pushed her back at arms lengths, but his hands remained on her shoulders. "Michele, we can't keep going on like this. I still love my wife, and I want her back…You and I, we've just been caught up in our emotions this past week. Do you understand what I am saying?"

A sinister grin crept across Michele's face. "So you still haven't told Carol about the boys or me yet?" She inched closer and closer to Jacob until she could feel the heat from his nostrils on her forehead.

"Uh, no. It's not the right time."

Her eyes narrowed in on him.

"You can't keep putting it off, J. Come clean with her and you'll find out that you two are over, and we can start our life together." She slowly licked her lips. She whispered, "Jacob, I know you want me." She guided his hand to her moist womanly mound.

His resistance was fading. "Michele, I, I, I still want to be with Ca…" He tried to pull away from her, but the massage she was giving to his now throbbing penis left him planted right in front of her.

In one swift movement, she dropped to her knees and began massaging his manhood with her mouth, lips, and tongue.

\*\*\*

"Carol, we made it to Friday." Mr. Martinez laughed as he carried Carol's bags to her car.

"Yes, we did. Our kids are great, so we don't have to deal with many of the issues other teachers deal with that have them pleading for Friday afternoons to arrive." Carol smiled as she hit the button on her key to unlock her car doors.

"Yeah, you're right." He placed the bags in the trunk of her SUV and let the hatch down. They stood face to face. "You sure you don't want to go to dinner tonight?"

"Eric…" Carol did not want to say the wrong thing. She enjoyed their conversations the past few nights that lasted from the moment she tucked the kids into bed until the sun almost came up. She missed sleep, but his calming spirit as they spoke on the phone was just what she needed to keep her mind off her current woes. "I…you know…." She rubbed her forehead in frustration.

He readjusted his bag on his shoulder and tucked his hands into his pockets. He tried not to sound as defeated as he felt. "Look, I know you're still technically married, but I can't help the way I feel about you. I have been attracted to you since the first day I met you, but once I found out you were married, I respected your union enough not to make any passes at you. Talking to you these past few days have been some of the best moments of my life this year." He put his bag on the ground to take some of the weight off of him. "You've said that you are going to divorce your husband, but you haven't yet taken any steps in that direction yet, so I'm not exactly sure if you will. All I know is that I really do care about you, and I want to explore us."

Carol was not shocked at his admission. There was something in the way he started and ended each conversation they had that let her in on his romantic interest in her. "Eric. If we were to have this conversation long after my divorce, I would be so willing to explore us, but right now I just can't. I've shared some things with you these past few days, but there is so much more that you don't know about that's going on in my life." Carol's shoulders slumped. "I have a lot to deal with before I can even begin to think about being involved with another man."

Eric understood, but it still did not lessen the blow he was being dealt. "Well, luckily for you I'm a patient man." They both laughed wryly. "If you'll allow me, I just want to be a friend to you and be there for you. If, and whenever, you are ready to take our friendship to another level, I'll be ready."

"Eric, I can't ask you to wait on me."

"You didn't." He smirked.

"Well, don't wait on me. You're such a great man and should be pursuing a woman who is ready to be there for you now and give you what you need now." Carol cast her eyes to the ground.

"You have your opinion and I have mine. Talk to you tonight?"

"Eric." Carol grinned.

"Tonight?"

"Okay." She got in her car and drove off.

\*\*\*

"Michele, I'm going to sit down there." Jacob pointed to the end of the first row after helping Michele to her seat.

Michele squeezed his hand. "Please sit here with me?"

Jacob loathed how needy and dependent Michele had become on him. He was just having sex with her, but he knew Michele was taking it for more than what it was; two people who leaned on each other sexually during trying times. He had every intention of winning Carol back so he would have to sever the most recent bond he formed with Michele soon; he just hoped that Carol would never find out about it. He sat next to Michele.

The service started with the minister praying for solace for the family. Michele's cousin sang a heart-wrenching rendition of "Precious Lord" in her Mahalia Jackson like voice, which left Jacob's lapel soaked with tears from Michele weeping on his shoulder. He knew she was in pain at the loss of her brother, but he noticed there was something in the way she would cry and then quickly recover to have sex with him or try to stir up conversation about them that made him really wonder about her; about her disorder.

Another one of Michele's cousins read the obituary while the congregation followed along silently. "Michael Jamar Robinson Jr. stepped into eternity on...." Cousin Donna's oratory was drowned out.

"Oh Lord, Lord why? My baby! My baby!" Michael's mother draped her body over his casket moaning and screaming.

"Come now. Come on, Mary. We'll get through this together." Michael Sr. pried his wife's body from the casket and escorted her back to her seat to help her regain her composure.

"And now we will have remarks from family and friends," the pastor said.

Michele was the first to stand. She pulled on Jacob to walk up there with her, but she went alone when she realized that he was intent on not going with her. She stood behind the podium and propped her elbows on it for support and took deep breaths as she dabbed at her face with Kleenex before she spoke, "hi, everyone." She feigned a smile. "I can't believe that I'm standing here today to give remarks, share memories of my brother, Michael, at his funeral." She inhaled and exhaled slowly. "It was just us two. I was his baby sister. He always seemed annoyed with me when we were younger, but I know that he cared for me like a big brother should."

Michele scanned the audience and spotted Carol a few rows up from the back of the church. Michele stood up straight. "Even though I moved to New York to live with my Aunt Tammy, he supported me through my pregnancy."

Carol's eyes widened. She shifted in her seat.

"Yes, I know many of you all don't know that I have twin boys, Joshua and Jacob Jr." She smirked and paused as if waiting for a response from the congregation.

Carol cleared her throat and sat completely erect in her seat.

"Michael played the father role as best as he could with my sons until they were finally united with their father, Michael's best friend, Jacob." Michele smiled and extended her hand in acknowledgment to Jacob. She looked up at Carol and smirked.

Carol gasped, but quickly covered her mouth to hide her shock. Her ears were burning. *Did she say what I think she just said?*

Jacob put his head down in shame and rubbed his forehead.

"I have so much to thank Michael for. He introduced me to Jacob Sr. in life, and he reunited us in his death. Thank you so much for being here for the kids, for me. We love you, and I know that you'll continue to be here to support me through this tragedy in my life." She looked at Jacob. Her eyes danced with admiration for him.

Jacob coughed and loosened his tie.

Carol could not take any more of Michele and her confession.

"Excuse me, excuse me, excuse me." She squeezed past the others in her row and ran out of the church.

Jacob turned to see what the commotion was at the back of the church only to see Carol storm out. He jumped up from his seat and ran after her.

Michele, with raised eyebrows and a sly smirk on her face, continued to share memories of her brother amidst her tears.

\*\*\*

"Carol. Carol. Carol. Wait. Slow down."

"Do not touch me." Carol did not care if he only grabbed her hand to stop her, his touch reminded her of the last time he touched her.

He held his hands up in surrender. "I'm sorry. Don't go."

"Why do you care? You've started another life with her." Carol's face was beet red.

"What?"

"Don't play dumb now. You've started a life with her and your twins, Joshua and Jacob Jr." Carol wiped tears from her eyes.

Jacob lowered his head.

Carol gripped her forehead. "Jacob Jr.? Not only do I find out at Mike's funeral that you have kids that I knew nothing about, but one of them has the nerve to be named Jacob Jr."

The brittle tone in Carol's voice signaled Jacob just how steaming mad and truly hurt she was.

"Carol, I'm sorry."

"Don't sorry me. How long have you known about them? Have you been raising them all of this time? Nope, don't answer that, because if you say something other than what Michele just confessed, I might slap you."

Jacob had never saw Carol this angry before.

"I swear Carol, I found out about them right before I lost my job. If I would've known that she had my kids eleven years ago, I would've told you that when we first met. I would've given you the chance to decide if you wanted to be with a man with kids. I definitely wouldn't have named our son Jacob Jr. too knowing that I already had one." Jacob wiped sweat from his forehead.

Carol screamed and threw her hands up in the air. "I can't believe this. Well, I hope you're happy with them, with her. Enjoy the rest of your life." Carol pivoted to walk away, but Jacob ran around in front of her to stop her exit.

"Jacob, move out of my way."

"Carol, I know that you're mad about this and still hurt from the other stuff I've done…"

"Stuff? Stuff? Say it. Say it. Say that you beat me. Say that you broke my ribs and blacked my eyes. Say it!"

Jacob jumped. "I'm sorry about the abuse baby, but we can work this out. We can go to counseling together. It can help us because it's been helping me. I'm learning how to deal with my anger. I swear that I will never hurt you again. I'm sorry. I need you. Let's work this out for the kids. For us. I love you." He looked deep into her eyes.

Carol's body tensed up, her forehead creased. "You love me? Not forgetting or forgiving you for what happened months ago, but you want me to add an affair…"

"An affair? I'm not having an affair." Jacob hoped the high pitch in his voice was not an indicator that he was lying.

"Yes, an affair. So I'm supposed to add it to the list of things to get over? Carol rubbed her stomach. "You expect me to believe that after the speech Michele gave and all the hints she threw out of how you've been there to 'support' her and the kids that you aren't sleeping with her? And oh, the kids. You have twin sons I knew nothing about, and you've kept them from me for only God knows how long. You think that I want you back? Are you serious?" Carol's hands flailed in the air as she spoke.

"I swear I'm not having an affair with Michele."

Carol clutched her abdomen. She took deep breaths trying to calm the pains in her stomach. "I don't believe you. Not at all." She walked away, but Jacob thwarted her attempt yet again. "Jacob, get out of my way." He was sleeping with another woman; she looked at him with such contempt in her eyes.

"I can't let you go. God, Carol, I miss you. I miss my kids." Jacob threw his hands up in the air. He rubbed his forehead and exhaled loudly.

"I don't care about you missing the kids!"

"Carol." Jacob took deep breaths as he learned in counseling to calm himself down. He exhaled slowly. "Not letting me see them has gone on long enough."

"You should've thought about them more when you were beating on me or while you were sleeping with her. I know you've been with her. I guess she's the one who's been texting me saying she was your first and now your last. I will not allow you to have my kids around her." Carol winced.

"If, if you keep this up…you'll force me to get the law involved to get joint custody… or full custody." Jacob threatened.

Carol's eyes almost bulged out of their sockets. "Ha! Good luck with that. I have pictures of my bruised face and X-rays of my broken ribs to prove that you might present a danger to my children. No judge will give you full custody." There was intense pressure in her head. Everything seemed to be spinning around her. She was cramping severely. She hunched over and clutched her stomach with both hands.

"Carol, are you okay?" Jacob touched her back.

"Get your hands off of me." Her arms flew up in defense to Jacob's touch.

Jacob was frightened. "Carol, you have blood dripping down your legs."

"What?" Carol looked down to see the blood flowing from under her dress. She fainted.

"Carol." Jacob caught her before her limp body hit the ground. He cradled her body next to his as he rushed to his car. He laid her across his backseat and sped off to the nearest hospital.

***

"Mr. Rodgers?" The doctor scanned the waiting room before he located the distraught man he assumed to be Jacob.

Jacob rushed up to him.

"Yes sir, how is my wife?" Jacob ignored the buzzing of his cell phone on vibrate in his pocket. He figured it was Michele calling or texting as she had been since a little after he ran out of the church after Carol.

"Well, we did everything we could to save the baby, but we just weren't able to."

"I'm sorry, did you say you weren't able to save the baby?" Jacob's forehead furrowed.

"Yes, she was a little over four months along. We did get her blood pressure stable. She's resting now. She's fine medically and can be discharged in a few hours, but in cases like this, we know the emotional trauma will take a long time to recover from."

Jacob needed to talk to Carol.

"Can I go in to see her now?"

"She may still be out of it, but you sure can."

The two men shook hands, and the doctor escorted Jacob to Carol's room.

Carol was lying on her side crying silently when Jacob entered.

"Carol." He moved towards her bed.

She rolled over. "Why are you still here?"

"Why wouldn't I be? You're my wife. We were talking one minute and the next you're bleeding, and you faint. I was scared."

Carol was too weak, physically and emotionally to put up a fight. She spoke calmly. "For one, we weren't talking, we were arguing, and two, I don't know what concern looks like from you anymore. You've put me through so much." Carol wiped her wet face.

"Carol, I don't want to upset you anymore, but why didn't you tell me that you were pregnant?"

"What was I supposed to say, Jacob I'm pregnant so let's get back together. You know I don't want you to hit me anymore, but if you do, I'll understand. Is that how I was supposed to tell you?"

Jacob put his head down.

"Maybe you would've threatened me to take away this baby too once you found out about him or her." A lump formed in Carol's throat. She cleared it and wiped her face.

Jacob spoke softly. "No, Carol, I wouldn't have."

"I don't know you anymore, Jacob. I don't know what you're capable of, but what I do know is that we will never be a family again." Carol rolled over, away from Jacob.

Jacob's phone rang again. He ignored it. The voicemail alert chimed. His text message alert chimed too.

Carol's phone buzzed too. She picked it up from the stand next to her bed. She checked the text message on her screen. *I don't care if he's with you, I had him first. He belongs to me.*

Carol kept her back turned towards Jacob. "You lied to me earlier. You said that you haven't been with Michele, but clearly you have, because no woman acts the way she does unless they have a reason to. Tell her to stop texting me about you. Tell her I'm not a threat to you all. You and I are over. She can have you." Carol closed her eyes.

Jacob sat next to Carol's bed for hours as she rested before he dozed off to sleep.

*\*\**

He awoke to his phone vibrating. He looked at the screen to see who it was. He braced himself before answering his phone. "Hello."

"What the hell have you done with Carol?" Sheila paced the floor. "I swear Jacob, if you hurt her again, you are a dead man."

"Sheila calm down. Carol and I were talking after the funeral. She fainted, and I brought her to the hospital."

"And with all of that happening, you didn't think to call me, her parents, her brother?"

"No, Sheila, I didn't. Everything happened so fast, besides, she's my wife. I know how to take care of her." Jacob was tired of being disrespected by Sheila.

"Calm down Sheila, just calm down," Sheila spoke to herself taking deep breaths. "I won't argue with you right now, just tell me that my friend is okay."

"Yes, she is."

The nurse entered.

"Look Sheila, I have to go."

"Don't hang up on me Jacob."

He ended the call.

"Mr. Rodgers, the doctor has discharged your wife. You are more than welcome to take her home now."

He wished that he could take her back to their home. "Thank you." Jacob started gathering Carol's belongings.

"Carol, Carol, wake up." He rubbed her forearm.

"Hunh?"

"You can go home now."

She rubbed her eyes. "I can?"

"Yeah."

"Okay." She pulled out her cell phone and googled a cab company.

Jacob wondered what she was searching for in her phone.

"Hello, yes is this Yellow Taxicab?"

"What are you doing?" Jacob questioned her.

She held her pointer finger up to silence him and continued to speak to the dispatcher.

"Carol, I'll take you home."

"Hold on a second please…" Carol turned to Jacob. "As in Sheila's home, right?"

Jacob let out a deep sigh. "Yes."

"I'm sorry to bother you, but I won't be needing your services." Carol ended the call and got dressed.

She would not let him push her in the wheelchair to the hospital exit doors. He had to walk ahead of her to the car because she refused to let him touch her and insisted that he not walk behind her for fear of what he could do to her with her back towards him.

They rode to Sheila's in silence.

Jacob pulled into the driveway and parked.

Carol opened her door, readying herself to jump out. "Thank you." She did not look in his direction as she spoke.

"Carol, wait."

"What is it now?"

"Can I please see my kids?"

"No, Jacob." She refused to look at him.

"Carol, how would you feel if someone kept you away from them?"

Carol finally faced Jacob. "Are you threatening me again?"

"No, no. All I'm asking is how you would feel if you hadn't been allowed to see them for the past four months…Think about that."

"I probably would go insane, I…"

"That's how I've felt." Jacob heaved a sigh. "Please just let me see them, hug them, kiss them and I promise I'll leave right away. We can talk about me seeing them again when you're more comfortable with it."

She lowered her head. She pursed her lips. "Okay."

Jacob smiled and jumped out of the car to open Carol's door. He looked at the house to see Sheila in the front room window staring at him. With her fist closed and thumb to her throat, she ran her hand in a slitting motion from one side of her throat to the other.

# *14*

Silence engulfed Edith and Edgar's home.

Not seeing their grands on a regular basis left a void in their interaction with one another.

Edgar spent most of the day in his workshop in the garage. He came in for dinner and retired nightly in the living room to watch reruns of 70's and 80's sitcoms.

Edith busied herself throughout the day knitting, cooking, playing Mahjong on the computer, and out in her garden.

"Edith?" Edgar had just come in from his workshop.

"I'm on the computer."

"I'm ready to eat." Edgar went and sat in his lazy boy chair and turned on the TV.

His plate was already prepared. She grabbed it from off of the stove and took it into the living room.

"Here." She placed his food on the TV tray in front of him.

She had eaten an hour earlier before he came in. She headed back to the computer to finish her game.

"Don't go. Sit with me."

Edith was taken aback by Edgar's request to sit with him. She obliged.

They laughed at Archie Bunker berate his son-in-law Michael on the sitcom *All in the Family.*

Edgar finished the last of his meal and turned the volume down on the TV. "You know, you remind me a lot of her." He smiled at Edith.

"Who?"

"Edith on the show, Archie's wife. She was so loving and forgiving and optimistic despite what they were going through. That was always something that I admired about you."

Edith was speechless. This was the most he had spoken to her in months.

"Edith, I'm not perfect. I never was." He kept his head low and smoothed out his eyebrows. "I did to you what I saw my father do to my mother. I probably would've kept beating on you had it not happened."

Edith knew exactly what "it" Edgar was talking about and sadness overwhelmed her. She cupped her mouth to prevent the sobs from echoing in the room.

Edgar turned to her and grabbed her hands. He held them tightly.

"Edith, I was stupid. I was selfish…I, I love our children more than life itself, I love you, so to know that my actions killed one of our children, our daughter." Edgar flicked at the tears rolling down his face.

Edith wept.

He wiped at her tears.

"That's why I went crazy when I found out that Jacob had been doing the same thing to Carol, my daughter! I already took one of my daughter's lives, I wasn't going to let another man do Carol the way I did you for all of those years. No, I wasn't going to let him take the only daughter that I have left."

Edith's hands were soaking wet with her tears. She shook her head remembering the agony of miscarrying her child, a girl, so late into her pregnancy. The baby would have been there third child.

Edgar's eyebrows furrowed. He shook his head at all of the pain he caused her.

"I should've stopped beating you long before I made you miscarry our daughter, better yet I should've never ever started hitting you at all." He pulled her closer to him, draping his arm across her shoulder. "I'm sorry, Edith, I'm so sorry…" Edgar's shoulders slumped as he cried.

Edith pulled him closer to her.

He knew he needed to say more to her. "I know that I hurt you, I just didn't know any better back then. Even after all of these years, I knew I was wrong, but I've just been too stubborn to admit that to you. Sometimes we can get so set in our ways and not know how to get out of our own way. I was wrong for putting my hands on you, night after night. Wrong for threatening you if you left with the kids when all you wanted to do was to get away from the mad man I was. I'm sorry for not really treating you the way you should've been treated."

Edith's breaths were choppy. Edgar grabbed her hand that was on his arm and kissed it.

Edith took a deep breath. She smiled.

"Edith, can you forgive me for all the hurt I've put you through?"

Edith sniffled. "I've waited for so long to hear you say those words to me. Yes, Edgar, I had to forgive you long ago, even without you asking for it. Being bitter toward you and resenting you would've hurt me more than you." She smiled. "But it feels so good to know that you're sorry."

Edgar stood up and pulled his wife to her feet. They stared into each other's eyes. Edgar leaned in and kissed Edith wildly.

"Edgar." Edith glowed.

"What? Can't a man kiss his wife?" He winked at her. "Come on, let's go to bed."

"Edgar." Edith cooed. She turned to walk, and Edgar smacked her on her butt.

They turned off all the lights in the house and made sure the doors were locked before they headed to their bedroom.

# *15*

"Ugh. This is too much." Michael's wife Rita flailed the insurance papers in one hand as she ended a call with the other.

"What is it, honey?" Michael's mother, Mary, asked. She continued to wash the dishes.

Rita sat at the island. "I was able to pay for the funeral arrangements from our savings account because I thought I would replace that money, plus more once the funds cleared from his insurance policy.

"Right, as we discussed. So what's wrong?"

"What's wrong is that the insurance company is saying they have to do a further investigation into the cause of the accident." She wiped her tears and tried to control her breathing.

Mary dried her hands with a dish towel and turned around to face Rita. "Investigation? Why do they need to do an—"

"Hey, what y'all up to?" Michele entered the kitchen. She grabbed a banana from the counter and peeled it open.

"Hey," Mary and Rita spoke one after the other.

"Sis, what's got you upset?" Michele bit into her banana.

Rita wiped at the constant flow of tears streaming down her face. She looked up at Michele. "The insurance company won't pay out yet on Michael's policy because they said they need an investigation done to determine the cause of the accident and his death."

Michele stood frozen. The banana dropped from her hand to the floor. There was a blank stare in her eyes.

"Girl, what is wrong with you?" Mary asked. Get that banana off the floor. You see me in here cleaning up."

"Michele?" Rita's eyebrows raised.

"Michele." Mary screamed at her again.

"Hunh? Hunh?" Michele came out of her trance.

"What has gotten into you?" Mary wiped the counter off from the banana chunks that fell out of Michele's gaping mouth.

"Oh, oh, nothing. You said they need to do an investigation into his death?" Michele wrung her hands behind her back.

"Yeah, they said that the police report came back and it appears to have been a homicide because the brake lines were cut."

Mary gasped and braced herself on the countertop.

Michele's pupils dilated. She fidgeted with her fingers and swallowed the lump in her throat before she spoke, "wh...why didn't the police tell us this sooner?" Michele fell back against the refrigerator and slid down to the floor.

"The car was so crunched up after the accident that it's taken them this long to tear it apart to see if there was anything faulty with the car. They found the brake lines cut. They determined the lines were literally cut with scissors and not damaged during the accident." She cupped her mouth to quell her moans.

Mary reached across the island to pass Rita a napkin. She then directed her attention to Michele. "Are you okay, honey?"

"Yeah." Michele looked up at Rita, hearing the agony in her cry. She struggled to refocus her thoughts. "I, I, I'm okay. I just can't believe that someone could've or would've even try to kill Michael. He's never done anything wrong to anyone." Michele jumped to her feet and ran crying from the kitchen to the bathroom to throw up.

"She has really been taking his death hard. Either she's all jolly chasing after Jacob or weeping looking at pics of Michael."

Rita shook her head. She stopped trying to wipe the tears from her eyes. There was a puddle of her tears on the countertop. The insurance papers were smudged. "I don't even care about the money at this point, I want to find out if he actually was murdered. Who did it? What for?" She slumped over the island and wailed.

Mary came around the island to rub Rita's back amidst wiping away her own tears.

\*\*\*

Michele flushed the toilet. She splashed cold water on her face. *No one was supposed to know.* She dropped her head and sobbed, refusing to look at her reflection in the mirror.

# *16*

Sheila had been avoiding Troy since that night she stormed from his apartment. Her heart had been paying for it ever since.

*Why do I feel this way about him? Why can't I just forget him like all the other men I've slept with?*

"Ugh." Sheila let out an audible sigh and picked up her cell phone. She needed to end things once and for all with Troy. He did not get the message that they were over when she stormed out the last time she saw him. Her lack of responding to his texts and calls was not getting through to him either. She was grateful that he was respectful enough to not just show up at her house. She needed to sit him down and talk to him one last time. Hopefully, she would convince him to move on.

She dialed his number and let his phone ring. "Hello, Troy?"

"Yes."

His tender voice weakened her resolve. *Stay strong Sheila.*

"Um, can we meet tonight? We need to talk."

"Sure."

"Okay great. How about we-"

"Sheila, I'll take care of everything. I'll text you the details, and you just make sure that you show up." Troy snickered.

"Okay." Sheila wondered how he took control of the situation so effortlessly.

***

"Hello, beautiful." Troy crooned as he kissed Sheila on her cheek.

"Hi, yourself." Sheila fought hard not to inhale his intoxicating scent. She leaned in to embrace him.

"This way." The maître d' escorted them to their seats. "Your waiter will be with you momentarily. Enjoy."

Troy pushed Sheila's seat in for her before he took his.

His stare commanded her eyes to look into his.

Sheila could not take it. One more second of staring into his eyes and she would be forced to admit to him the hold he had on her heart. *No! I came here to wish him well with his life and future, not tell him I love him.* Sheila cleared her throat and took a sip of her wine. "So Troy, how have you been?" She figured small talk might soften the blow of what she needed to say.

He laughed. "I know you didn't come here for small talk. Say what you need to say before I say what I have to say."

*If there were any man I would give my heart to, it would be him. He is so sure of himself. I love that about him....Okay, focus Sheila. He wants the truth, so give it to him.* She squared her shoulders. She averted direct eye contact with him.

"Look Troy, clearly you didn't hear me the last time I saw you when I told you that I couldn't do this with you. I'm not the marrying type, hell I'm not the relationship type, so do yourself a favor and move on. I can't and won't love you like you want, need, and deserve." She lowered her head and fidgeted with the napkin on her lap.

He laughed inwardly at her. "Sheila-"

"Hello, my name is John and I'll be your waiter for the evening. May I start you off with-"

"John, we know exactly what we want." Troy gazed at Sheila.

Sheila retreated further back into her seat under Troy's intense stare at her.

They gave John their order, he grabbed their menus and left. Troy stared at her with such intensity in his eyes.

Sheila sipped more of her wine. "You were saying?"

He laughed at her again. She was trying so hard to keep her guard up with him. "I've shared with you that I want you in my life and why. You told me that you didn't want me in your life, but I don't believe you. We don't just have sex, we make love. I don't believe you kiss or touch a man the way you do me unless you have real feelings for him." His stare softened even more. "I wish you would tell me about it or let go of whatever it is from your past that's keeping you from giving us the chance we deserve." He reached out and caressed her hand.

She let the warmth and strength of his hand cover hers before she pulled back and placed it on her lap. She opened her mouth to speak, but could not find the words to say. *Get it together Sheila. You know what you came here to do. You cannot let this fine man break down your resistance, you are strong girl.*

"Sheila, talk to me."

"Troy." Sheila could not believe her emotions were betraying her. She quickly wiped away the tear that was falling along her cheek. "I don't think this was a good idea meeting you tonight. I'm sorry. I have to go." Sheila jumped from her seat to leave, but Troy's firm, yet gentle grip on her wrist comforted her to stay.

Tears streaked her face. He reached across the table and began to stroke her face and brush away the tears as they fell from her eyes.

She allowed her head to rest in his hand. She took deep breaths and sniffled.

He came around to her and knelt beside her. "Sheila, whatever happened in your past, we can get through it, over it, whatever we need to do, let's just do it together.

*Don't do it. You can't trust men.* She looked into his eyes. "Okay." *I'll stay for just one more round of sex with him, but then it's definitely over.*

He kissed her lips softly and returned to his seat.

The waiter returned with their food and placed each of their meals in front of them. "Bon Appetit."

\*\*\*

"Good morning, night crawler. Boy, are you glowing."

"Whatever." Sheila laughed as she grabbed orange juice from the refrigerator. She sat on a bar stool at the kitchen island.

"So you left out last night saying you were going to tell Troy to leave you alone and then return home to watch movies with me." Carol feigned sadness.

"Sorry, girl. I had business to take care of." Sheila popped a grape in her mouth.

Carol leaned over the countertop with her head resting on her hands. "Well?"

"Well, what?"

"What did you tell him? That you love him and will give him a chance?" Carol's eyes brightened.

"Girl, bye." Sheila laughed. "I made him think that I would give us a chance, but I only did that to get sex from him." Sheila buckled over in laughter.

"You should be ashamed of yourself." Carol shook her head and smacked her lips at Sheila.

"Okay, enough about me, what about you? We haven't talked about you know what?"

"What is there to talk about? I was pregnant one minute and the next I wasn't." Carol busied herself wiping off the countertop.

"Carol, that's a big thing honey, I think you need to talk about it, deal with it."

"You want me to talk about it, but you won't deal with whatever happened from your past that has your opinion of men so jacked up." Carol stared at Sheila.

Sheila turned her back to Carol and wiped her eyes. She was tired of her Uncle Tommy issues affecting her.

Carol came around the counter. She pulled Sheila's hands away from her face. "I'm sorry, Sheila." She pulled Sheila into her arms. "I didn't mean to be so nasty."

"I know you didn't." Sheila sniffled.

Carol rubbed Sheila's back. "It's just something that I need to deal with in my own time." Carol stepped back from Sheila to look her in her eyes. "Yes, I'm hurt over losing the baby, but I'm trying to convince myself that it happened for a reason. I don't know what the heck that reason is, and I hope in time I'll find out, but I'm trying to trust that things turned out the way they were supposed to." Carol wiped her eyes.

"I'm sorry." Sheila looked up smiling.

"It's okay. When I'm ready to talk about it, I know that I have a listening ear with you, just like you should know, whenever you're ready to deal with your past, I'm here for you. No judgment."

"You better not judge me."

They both laughed.

"So, since I ditched you last night, did you spend it chatting with Eric? I think he would be great for you." Sheila piled some of the breakfast Carol was making onto her plate.

"I did chat with him for a while." Carol smiled. "But as far as him being great for me, hello, earth to Sheila, I'm still married."

"Not for long though, right? When are you going to file for a divorce?"

Carol averted eye contact with Sheila.

"It's been over five months. You left him because he was beating on you, and then you found out that he was cheating on you, might I add with his baby momma. If that ain't enough reason to send you running to get a divorce, then I don't know what will." Sheila threw her hands up in the air.

"I thought you just told me not to judge you, but it sounds like that's what you're doing to me." Carol crossed her arms at her chest and stared at Sheila.

Sheila hurried up chewing the food in her mouth. "I'm not judging you. It's just that I want you to use your head with this one. You deserve so much more than what you were given." Sheila's eyes pleaded for forgiveness from Carol.

Carol rolled her eyes but smiled. "Yeah, whatever." They both laughed.

"Everything is not so simple, Sheila. I hate what he did to me, but I have kids to think about. Would it be best for them if Jacob and I got divorced? And besides, it's not like I'm not 100% sure that Jacob has been with Michele."

Sheila bucked her eyes and neck at Carol in amazement. She was speechless.

"Just hear me out. She just seems evil and will do anything to get Jacob, even if that means lying about being with him to drive a further wedge between us. I don't know. I still need more time to think about everything."

Sheila stared incredulously at Carol. "I'm going to pretend like I didn't hear what you just said and attempt to have a pleasant conversation with you over breakfast."

Carol squinted at Sheila. "What?"

"So you're also going to ignore the fact that he knew that he had kids with her and never bothered to tell you that? And don't tell me that 'he just learned about them' story. It doesn't matter if he knew all along or just found out. The minute he knew, you were supposed to know. You were not some random chick, you were his wife...still are, according to you." Sheila shook her head but laughed.

"I can't stand you." Carol rolled her eyes.

"Yeah, but you love me." Sheila smiled. "We need to change the subject before I go crazy talking about this foolishness. So, what are your plans for today?"

"Well, I'm going to take the kids to my parents' house while I go meet with Jacob."

Carol waited for Sheila to verbally attack her about her decision to meet with Jacob, but Sheila sat quietly.

Carol drew strength from Sheila's silence and decided to continue talking. "Ironically both Jacob Jr.'s birthdays are the same day. J.J. really wants his dad at his party and Jacob expressed to me that their mother wanted to have a big birthday party for the twins that same day."

Sheila almost choked on her orange juice from laughing so hard. "So, you can't even call the woman by her name, she's just 'their mother' but you're telling me you don't think Jacob has been with her? Haa. Okay. Carry on."

"I'm just meeting with him today to talk about little J.J's party."

"Aw ok, have fun." Sheila pursed her lips.

Carol laughed.

"What's funny?"

"Nothing, just thinking. What if he asks if we can have the boys' parties together so that he can be at both? What would you think of that?" Carol really did want Sheila's opinion.

"No comment." Sheila pretended to zip her lips, lock them, and throw away the key. She emptied her plate in the garbage can and headed to bed. She had been up all night.

"Sheila. Don't be that way."

"Yeah, whatever," Sheila called out as she ascended the stairs.

***

"Oh, my grands. I've missed you so much." Edith squeezed Kaylee and J.J. as tight as she could, pinched their cheeks, and planted kisses all over their faces.

146

They giggled.

"We missed you, too." Kaylee exhorted.

"Gramps." Kaylee screamed and jumped into Edgar's arms when he came from the kitchen.

He held her tightly, put her down, then picked up J.J. and did the same.

Carol wiped the tears from her eyes as she smiled.

"Mom, dad... I'm sorry for keeping the kids away from you all for so long."

Edith walked over to Carol. "It's okay honey, we're just glad that you're okay, they're okay. We're so happy to see you all." Edith hugged Carol.

"Dad." Carol held her arms out as she rushed into his open arms.

"I love you, sweetie." He kissed her forehead.

"I love you too, dad. Thanks for watching the kids while I go meet with Jacob."

"Carol?"

"Yeah, dad?"

"Don't hesitate to call me if you even think that he might try to harm you while you're with him."

"Thanks, dad, but I don't think that will happen again."

"Just don't hesitate to call if you need me or your brother."

"I won't."

"Come on grands, let's go in the kitchen and see what snacks I have for you."

"Yay." Kaylee and J.J. jumped and shouted in in sync.

\*\*\*

"Thanks for meeting me here." Jacob stood as Carol approached the table.

He asked her to meet him at Panera Bread. He chose a table outside to enjoy the sunny day. His phone buzzed. He ignored it and continued discussing the plans for the party with Carol. His phone buzzed again. He ignored it.

Carol shook her head. "You better answer it or at least text her back before she goes crazy on you."

Jacob was sweating. "What are you talking about?"

"Don't what me. I know it's her. Don't make your girlfriend wait any longer." Carol turned her head and stared aimlessly at the park across the street. Her eyes zoomed in on a family that reminded her of the one she once had with Jacob. She frowned.

Jacob leaned in closer. "Carol, I told you nothing is going on between Michele and me. She's planning the twins' party as well, so she's just been updating me. That's all."

Jacob wished he did not have to lie to Carol. He wished he would have never slept with Michele at all.

"Carol?"

"What?" She sipped some of her iced tea and smoothed out her skirt.

"What if we had all of the boys' party together?"

Carol buckled over in laughter.

"Carol, what's so funny?"

She stifled her laughter to speak. "That you would even ask me that." She continued laughing.

"I'm being serious though."

"That's the funny and sad part about it. After all that has happened, especially her broadcasting the fact that you are the father of her children, at her brother's funeral for God's sake, you would think that I would even consent to having a party together for her boys and my son." Carol's nostrils flared as her eyes zoomed in on Jacob.

He wiped sweat from his forehead and cleared his throat. "Carol, I know you may think that I'm being insensitive to your feelings or what has happened between us, but putting that aside, this day is supposed to be all about the boys. They're going to meet anyway. Why not do it in a fun way like a birthday party?"

Carol put her head down and tapped her foot trying to calm her nerves.

Jacob continued speaking. "I've always been at J.J.'s birthday parties and I don't want to risk the chance of missing it, trying to be at my other sons' party." Jacob sat back and sighed.

"Although I don't care about your feelings right now, I hear what you're saying." Carol sighed.

"Thanks."

"Don't thank me just yet, because I still won't agree to have a party for my son with her there." Carol pursed her lips.

"Carol—"

"No." Carol pointed at Jacob. "The way she humiliated me that day at the funeral. The constant texts I get from her about you two and leaving you alone, I will not tolerate that around my kids." She wagged her finger.

"Carol, this has to happen at some point."

"Not at this point in my life." Carol slammed her hand on the table.

Jacob was taken aback by the Carol sitting in front of him. She had become more vocal. "Carol, you've changed."

"I have you to thank for that." She pointed at him.

He sat at the edge of his seat. "Carol, I know that I don't have the right to demand much from you at this point."

"You don't have the right to demand anything from me."

Jacob lowered his head in defeat. "I know that, but I can't change the fact that I do have children with her and that those children, my sons Joshua and Jacob Jr., need to meet Kaylee and J.J." He shook his head at the thought of having two juniors.

"Say it. Say that one Jacob Jr. needs to meet the other Jacob Jr." Carol tried to contain her tears, but she was just so frustrated and hurt that one tear escaped and rolled down her face.

"Carol, I'm sorry."

"Yes, you are." She wiped her wet face.

Jacob scooted to the edge of his chair. "Carol, I know it's weird that there are two Jacob Jr.'s, but like I told you before, if I would've known about the twins, you would have too, and I never would've named our son Jacob as well."

"Yeah, well there's nothing we can do about that because I'm certainly not changing my son's name." Carol sat back and folded her arms across her chest.

Jacob sat back doing the same.

They sat in silence for what seemed like an eternity.

"Carol, I know this is not the life you had in mind for you and I, for the kids, but because of things I did knowingly and unknowingly, we find ourselves here. We need to put our kids first. Make decisions with their best interest in mind."

Carol's eyebrows raised. Her head swayed. "First of all, I already made all of the arrangements for J.J's party, but considering the fact that you are his father, I decided to go over the details with you. Despite how I feel about you, I want to do what's best for my son."

"Our son." Jacob furrowed his eyebrows.

"Yeah, that. I know as young as he is, he would be sad not to have you there. And what's best for my kids is to not be thrown in a lion's den. I mean what if the twins don't like Kaylee and J.J.? God only knows what their mother has been saying to them about you, about me. I won't just stand by and watch your boys mistreat my children." Carol's blood boiled at the mere thought of that happening.

"Carol, I can reassure you that won't happen. I have talked to the boys. They're not mad at me because they know that I didn't know about them. They aren't angry or bitter, in fact, they are happy to have me around."

"Just like their mother." Carol rolled her eyes.

Jacob ignored her snide remark and continued talking, "I've talked to them about Kaylee and J.J. and they really want to get to know the kids. They think it's kind of cool to have a little brother to play with and a little sister to protect."

Carol shook her head. "So the boys might be fine about it, but I'm certain Michele isn't. I know she doesn't like me. If I even catch her looking funny at my kids…" Carol's eyes narrowed, and her nostrils flared.

"Calm down Carol. I don't think Michele would do anything to harm Kaylee or J.J., remember, she's a mother too."

Carol crossed her arms at her chest again.

Jacob's phone rang.

Carol shook her head at him.

His voicemail alert chimed.

Carol rested her head in her hands as she leaned on the table. She looked back and forth from Jacob to his phone suggesting with her eyes that he respond to it.

His phone rang again.

Carol grabbed his phone.

"Hello, Michele."

"Who is this?"

"This is Carol."

"Carol?" Michele's eyes widened. Her pupils danced. "Let me speak to Jacob."

"My husband and I are taking care of business, so-"

Michele interrupted Carol. "Stop acting like you two are getting back together. You two are only discussing your son's birthday." Michele laughed.

"Don't kid yourself." Carol smirked.

Jacob reached for his phone from Carol, but she scooted her chair back putting more distance between them.

"Oh, whatever. It's my sons' birthday that day too. I should be there for the planning too." Michele smacked her lips.

"No, you don't have the right to be here. Jacob and I need to finish discussing our son's party, so if you don't mind, which I wouldn't care if you did." Carol pulled the phone away from her ear and stared at the phone in pity and disgust as if Michele could see her expression before she put it back up to her face. "Can you stop calling him? I'm sure he'll get back to you when he's ready to."

"Ex-"

Carol ended the call with Michele still talking. She powered Jacob's phone off.

He sat back staring at her with wide eyes and raised eyebrows.

Carol sat back in her seat shaking her head. "Honestly, I toyed with the idea of a joint party before I got here, for the sake of the kids, but that right there is a perfect example of why she's not allowed to be at my son's party." She slid Jacob a piece of paper with the address to where the party would be. She put her sunglasses on, pursed her lips at Jacob staring him up and down, and then left.

Jacob sat helpless as he watched the love of his life walk away, again.

## *17*

"Carol, you picked a great space. The kids are going to have so much fun running around here, playing and jumping on all these inflatables." Edith smiled.

"Yeah how did you find out about this place?" Sheila asked.

"One of my coworkers told me how much fun her three-year-old son and his friends had here, so I figured it would be a great place for J.J's party." She smiled as she watched him go down the pirate ship's slide. She looked over to see Kaylee bouncing in the Disney Princess's playpen.

"These people are really smart." Sheila nibbled on some candy that Carol laid out on the treats table.

"What people?" Carol laughed.

"The ones who set this place up. They have so many inflatables for the kids to play in. And girl, even better, they have workers to interact with the kids while the parents and adults chill in this great comfy space." Sheila fell back on to one of the leather couches in the corner they were in.

Carol had reserved that section because from it she would always be able to see the kids no matter what inflatable they chose to play on.

"Oh, those people." Carol laughed and continued to arrange the snacks and Mickey Mouse decorated birthday cake on the table for the kids. She ordered pizza from the facility so she would call the kids over in another hour or so to sing happy birthday and eat before she let them go back and play a while longer.

"Where is Jacob?" Edith asked.

"He-"

"Yeah, where is he? He's been so adamant on seeing the kids, so why isn't he here yet?" Sheila snapped.

"You wouldn't even let me answer my mother before you started growling." Carol laughed.

Sheila rolled her eyes but laughed.

"He said he's picking up something special for J.J., but they didn't have it ready when he got there, so he decided to wait for it. He said he would be like twenty minutes late."

"Okay."

Carol leaned into Sheila. "I know what he did, but why are you more hostile where Jacob is concerned than I am?"

Sheila's eyebrows furrowed. "Because I know what he did."

"I'm not saying that I forgive him for what he did, but you blow up at him more than I do."

"I know he abused you, but when he did that, he hurt me too. Sheila leaned in closer to Carol. "He betrayed my trust in him too. I introduced you to him. The three of us have been so close all these years and to find out he did all of this to you." Sheila wiped the one tear that escaped her eye. "I looked up to him. I thought he had my back, would be there to protect me from some nut if need be, but who was there to protect you from him."

Carol reached over and hugged Sheila.

"This is supposed to be J.J.'s day, not Sheila-bearing-her-soul day."

There was a commotion at the door.

They both laughed, but quickly looked up to see what was going on.

A man was trying to keep a woman from coming through the door.

Sheila stood up to get a better look at what was going on. Carol stood up beside her.

Carol knew that the man with his back facing her trying to usher the woman out the door was Jacob.

Sheila snapped her neck in Carol's direction. "I clearly see that that's Jacob, but is that Michele trying to barge her way in here?"

Carol was dumbfounded.

"You want me to handle this for you?" Carol's brother Mark came and stood next to her huffing.

"No, Mark. Please behave yourself today. We cannot make a scene in front of the kids. They don't know what's going on between their father and I and I want to keep it that way for as long as I can."

"Okay, lil sis. I'll go over there with the kids and try to keep them occupied, but trust me, I have my eye on him. If he so much as stares at you too long, I'll be more than glad to handle him again." His jaws clenched and his fists tightened.

"And I'll be right there if you need me, tiger." Sheila smiled and playfully punched Mark in the arm.

He smiled and kissed Sheila on the cheek, but growled when he looked back in Jacob's direction. He walked off towards the kids.

Michele managed to rush past Jacob at the same time little J.J. spotted him.

"Daddy, daddy, daddy." Little J.J. ran up to Jacob with his arms up in the air jumping up and down for his dad to pick him up.

Jacob obliged him.

"Hey, little man." He squeezed him as tight as he could.

The twins stood next to Michele.

"Ma, can we go play?"

"You sure can." Michele smirked at Carol across the room.

The twins ran off towards the alligator inflatable.

Sheila charged towards Michele, but Carol grabbed her wrist and snatched her back next to her. "Sheila, calm down. Please do not make a scene here."

"Me make a scene? That heifer already started the play, I just want to move on to the next scene, all over her head."

"Sheila."

"Okay, alright, okay. I'll calm down for now, but I can't guarantee how I'll act for much longer." Sheila walked towards the wall behind her. She was talking to herself to calm herself down when firm hands wrapped around her waist.

"Who in the…" She turned, prepared to go off on the stranger that dared to touch her, instead she found herself staring into Troy's brown eyes.

"Tr…Troy, what are you doing here?" She smoothed her hair down and rubbed her lips together to make sure they both were glossy.

He smiled.

"Your lips are fine."

They both laughed.

"You've been avoiding me."

"No, I haven't." She put her head down.

He laughed. "You had me thinking that night at dinner that we were all good. I took you back to my house, and we made love the way only you and I-"

"This is not the place to be discussing us and what we do." Sheila pursed her lips. "And how did you know I was here anyway?"

"You've always been so cute when you act all tough." Troy smiled and pecked Sheila on her nose. "And remember, you told me about not being available for me today because it was J.J's birthday."

Sheila tapped her chin with her finger. She feigned being confused.

"Well, when I called Carol to wish him a happy birthday, she told me that I was more than welcome to come. So here I am. Tadow." Troy extended his arms and laughed.

Sheila was about to lay into Troy when little J.J. ran up to them.

"Uncle Troy, Uncle Troy."

"Hey, little man." He rubbed his head.

"Come, come play with me." J.J. pulled hard on Troy's hand.

Sheila spoke low. Her eyes became beady as she zoomed in on Troy. "Go play with him, we'll talk later."

Troy ran off with J.J.

Sheila headed back over towards Edith.


Jacob was still stationed near the front door. "Michele, why did you come here?"

"Because this is a public place, and I knew the boys would have fun here, so I brought them." She smirked.

"But you knew that this is where J.J's party would be today." Jacob blew his breath out hard in frustration.

"And? It's also the twins' birthday, so I wanted them to have some morning fun before their party this evening."

"Can you just leave, please? I'll see you and the boys later."

"No, I will not leave. This is a public place. I paid for the boys and I to come in here and have fun, and that's what I'll let them do until they get ready to leave." She left him standing there and sashayed past Carol, Sheila, and Edith. She sat at a table far across from them. She smiled as she pulled out her phone to search the internet.

Carol stood by the birthday cake, baffled that Michele had shown her face there.

Jacob walked over to Carol.

"So that's her?" Edith tilted her chin into her chest to look above her eyeglasses. "Her over there in that adult onesie. That light-skinned woman over there with that long wavy hair and those short shorts."

"Haaa. Momma Matthews you are too funny." Sheila kissed Edith's cheek. "You said she has an adult onesie on." Sheila buckled over with laughter in her seat.

Edith swatted at Sheila. "Knock it off." Edith laughed low.

"I don't normally talk about people, but you would think she would have the decency to put on some clothes knowing she would be around all these kids." Edith shook her head.

"Key word: decency. She lacks that." Sheila rolled her eyes in Michele's direction. Sheila leaned into Edith and whispered to her, forcing Edith to laugh relentlessly.

"Jacob, get away from me now." Carol spoke through clenched teeth and under her breath as she put pizza on the plates for the kids. She took deep breaths to even her breathing; she did not want

Michele to see the effect her presence was having on her.

Jacob moved closer to her. "Carol, I'm sorry. I didn't invite her. I know how you felt about her-"

"Lower your voice." Carol hushed him over her shoulder. She continued laying out the food.

"Here sweetie, let me help you." Sheila grabbed the spatula from Carol's trembling hands. She barked at Jacob.

Carol finally turned to face Jacob. "I am so tired of your sorrys. You've ruined our marriage, my life, and now J.J.'s birthday party."

He took a deep breath to calm his nerves and not appear hostile to Carol. "I know you're tired of hearing it, but I am sorry, and I have changed. Yes, she's here. No, I didn't invite her. See, she's sitting over there quietly. I asked her to leave, but she wouldn't. So let's just enjoy the rest of our son's birthday party." He smiled at her as a peace offering.

Little J.J. ran up to them huffing, puffing, and crying holding his eye.

Carol swooped down to pick him up. "J.J. what's wrong with you?"

His words could barely be understood through his tears.

The twins ran over to Jacob.

Little J.J. reached out for his daddy to grab him.

Carol held on to him for as long as she could before she admitted to herself that he would much rather his daddy console him.

"Daddy's little man, stop crying." Jacob brushed away J.J.'s tears. "Tell me what's wrong."

J.J. managed to stifle his tears, but still held his eye as he spoke. "The big boy did a back flip and he kicked me in the eye." He turned and pointed to the other Jacob Jr. standing next to his dad.

"I'm sorry dad, Mr. Jacob, I didn't mean to, I swear I didn't. I didn't even know he was right there until I heard him crying." He looked genuinely remorseful.

Michele stomped heading in their direction.

"How could you not see him?" Carol directed her statement to the big Jacob Jr. but patted little J.J.'s back.

"You're sorry?" J.J.'s teary eyes looked into his older brother's.

"Yeah, I am."

"Well, it's okay then." J.J. continued to rub his eye, but his cries stopped.

"What is going on over here?" Michele sandwiched herself in between her sons.

"Nothing, everything is okay." Jacob tried to assuage her.

Sheila walked up and Troy was close behind her.

"If there is something going on over here Jacob, please let me know." Michele moved closer to him.

"Your son kicked my son in the eye." Carol bucked her eyes at Michele.

"I wasn't talking to you, I was talking to the father of my children." Michele turned her head from Carol to look at Jacob.

"Michele everything is ok. You can go back over there." Jacob urged her.

"No, I won't. I won't stand by while she accuses my son, Jacob Jr. of being malicious."

Little J.J.'s eyes lit up. "His name is Jacob Jr. too, daddy?"

Michele rested her arms on Jacob Jr. "Yes, honey. He was born first." Michele spoke to little J.J.

"Don't speak to my son." Carol tried to snatch J.J. from Jacob, but he held on to him tightly.

Mark walked over and stood next to Carol.

"I didn't say anything wrong to him, but I heard the way you talked to my son, you owe him an apology." Michele folded her arms, shifted onto one leg, and stared at Carol.

"I don't—"

"Give him to me." Edith grabbed J.J. from Jacob and ushered the twins and the other kids away from the volatile adults.

"I'm waiting." Michele pursed her lips and tapped her foot.

"You'll be dead before you know it waiting on an apology from her. She doesn't owe you a thing." Sheila stepped out in front of Carol.

"And who are you?"

"Your worst nightmare if you don't leave now."

"Sheila, calm down."

"You better shut up talking to me, Jacob." Sheila snarled.

"Oh, so you're Sheila. Good job keeping her company." Michele pointed at Carol. "While I entertain him." She winked at Jacob.

Jacob shook his head.

"You better get that finger out of my face."

"It ain't in your face, but if it was, what would you do?" Michele put her finger in Sheila's face.

Sheila punched Michele right in her face but was not able to finish what she had planned because Troy pulled her back, and Jacob got in between them coaxing Michele back.

"Let me go. Let me go. She just can't hit me and get away with it." Michele swung at Sheila trying to escape Jacob's grasp.

Troy used all of his energy to subdue Sheila. She was really strong.

"Get off of me, Jacob. I am tired of this. Have the past few weeks not meant anything to you?" Michele feigned being hurt.

"Not now, Michele. Not now." Jacob eyes widened. He cocked his head and tightened his lips staring at Michele.

Carol stood frozen. She could not believe J.J.'s birthday had been ruined at the hands of the tramp in front of her.

Troy continued using all of his strength to keep Sheila from charging at Michele.

"Not now, not now, not now, that's all that I've been hearing. When will my now come? When will you tell Carol that you and I have been seeing each other? She left you, why should she care anyway." Michele poked her head out from around Jacob to stare at Carol.

"Oh, you can take this beat down now." Sheila charged at Michele causing Mark to step in to help Troy hold her back.

"Come on." Michele allowed her body to lean in to Jacob's.

"Oh, I can show you better than I can tell you." Sheila took off running like a track star with her fists balled towards Michele. She used all of her might to try and escape Troy, but his hold on her waist was too strong.

"Enough!" The veins in her forehead throbbed. Carol was seething with anger. She stepped in front of Sheila. "You said that everything would be okay today. You told me over and over again that you weren't with her, but you lied to me yet again." The solid look of disgust in her eyes cut Jacob to his core. "I hate you." Carol stormed off to the get the kids.

Michele smirked. She slowly peeled herself off of Jacob.

"Jacob, get her out of here now, before I..." Sheila was struggling to get out of Troy's grip.

Michele turned to respond to Sheila's threat but spotted the gentleman with her. "Troy?"

"Michele?" Troy could not believe it was Michele Robinson.

"What are you doing here?" Michele's eyebrows raised.

Sheila threw up her hand wagging her pointer finger. "Never mind what he's doing here, how do you know him?"

Michele grinned. "Wouldn't you like to know."

Sheila broke away from Troy. She turned to look him directly in the face. "How do you know her?"

Troy was flustered. "Sheila, I...we..."

"Oh cut the dramatics. You must not know him that well if you didn't know that he and I were together for two years when he lived in New York. Oh, so you're the one." Michele giggled.

"The one? The one what?"

"The one that couldn't satisfy him, so he turned to me." Michele winked at Sheila. "But don't worry, my heart wasn't with him." She pointed to Troy. "It's always been with him." She smiled and tried to wrap her arms around Jacob's neck, but he quickly pulled back from her avoiding her grasp.

Sheila charged at Michele, but Troy held her back.

"Let me go." Sheila cut Troy with her eyes.

He let her go.

She flew out of the building right after Carol.

Troy chased after Sheila.

Edith and Edgar grabbed their belongings and left.

Mark shook his head in shame and disgust at Jacob as he carried the car seat with his infant baby girl in one hand and held his wife's hand with the other and headed out the door.

Jacob shook his head and stared at Michele.

"What? What did I do?"

He fell back on the couch behind him and covered his face.

Michele grinned.

# *18*

*It's settled, Jacob and I are getting a divorce. Sheila tried to tell me that he was sleeping with Michele, but I just didn't want to accept it. As much as he hurt me with the physical abuse, I guess there was some small part of me that was still hoping that we might reconcile one day, but that part of me is dead. It's time to put my life back together and move on.*

Carol's phone rang.

"Carol?"

"Hi, mom."

"How are you doing sweetheart?"

"I'm good. Just thinking about some things and making some decisions."

"Oh, like what?"

"Well." Carol exhaled a deep breath. "I've decided that it is time to file for a divorce from Jacob."

"Are you sure that's what you want to do?" Edith winced, considering all that happened at the birthday party yesterday.

"Yes. I have to. I've been staying with Sheila for too long now. I think that it's definitely time to get my own place. Get into the routine of it just being me and the kids."

"Carol, it'll never just be you and the kids. You have your father and me, Mark, and obviously Sheila. You will never be alone."

"I know mom, but I'm saying it'll just be me and the kids under the same roof alone."

"Honey, you know that you can stay with us. We would love to have the grands around here every day."

"I know mom, and I thank you for the offer, but I need my own place. Do you understand?" Carol hoped she did not offend her mother.

"I understand sweetie. So do you have any idea where you're planning to move?"

"Not yet. Somewhere I can afford, near my job, and safe and comfortable enough to raise the kids. As soon as I get off the phone with you I'm going to search some sites for a place."

"Well, you're always welcome to come stay with us. We have enough space, but I understand you wanting to be on your own, you always were independent like that. You are so strong, and I am so proud of you. I love you."

"Thanks, mom. I love you too."

Carol hung up the phone. She was ready to search for a place to live, but her phone rang again.

"Hi, Eric. How are you?" She sat Indian style on the patio chair.

"I'm good. How are you?"

"I'm…let's just say that I have had a very interesting weekend."

"Do you want to talk about it?"

"No, not now. Maybe one day I'll be able to share the most recent sordid details of my life." She sighed. "The conversation is always focused on me, how about you, how are you doing?"

"I'm good, just getting mentally prepared to get back into the swing of things for the new school year starting next Monday."

"Right. To add to me going back to work full-time, I have to find a place to live."

Eric knew from his talks with Carol that she was not on the best terms with her husband, but he wondered to what extent. Were they really over? "You and your husband getting a bigger place?"

Carol paused. *How much should I tell him? Should I change the subject?* "Ummmm, no, it'll just be me and the kids moving into this new place."

Eric smiled. *I might have a chance with Carol, after all.* "Carol, you know that you can talk to me if you need to."

"Thanks, Eric, for being such a good friend, but I'm not ready to talk about it yet, still sorting some stuff out in my head, you know?"

"I understand."

"Thanks." She smiled. "Well, I have to go check up on the kids. I have so many things that I need to take care of this week, so if I don't get a chance to chat with you this week we can always catch up the first day back at work. Take care."

"Ok. You too…goodnight."

Carol used Google as the search engine on her laptop. She opened up two windows: one for an apartment search and the other, a divorce lawyer.

# *19*

It had been two weekends since the boys' birthday party, and Sheila had managed to avoid Troy.

This time around in hopes of getting her back, he stopped by her house, but luckily for Sheila, Carol was there and spoke on Sheila's behalf.

Carol opened the door to take a bag of clothes out to her truck and bumped into Troy.

"Oh, I'm sorry Troy. I didn't mean to-"

"Don't worry about it. Let me help you to your car." Troy gathered the clothes that fell out of the bag, put them back in the bag Carol had and carried it to the car for her.

"Thanks. Look Troy, you've been stopping by and calling her for the past two weeks trying to get her to see things your way, but she's not trying to hear any of it now. I know Sheila. Yes, she can be stubborn as ever, please don't tell her that I told you this." Carol smiled with her hands in a praying position. "But, she honestly, truly does care about you. She's just not sure if she can trust you, especially since you were with…" A snarl formed on Carol's lips. "I believe if you give her some time, she'll come around."

Troy smiled.

"Do you think you could at least get her to listen to me so that she can have the full story of Michele and I's past while she is thinking things over?"

"Well, she's helping me move to my place today, so now isn't the best time." Carol really wanted to get her stuff from Sheila's over to her new place before the heat of the day set in.

"I understand. Need my help?"

"I would love it, but you two in close proximity might not be so great. She's still pretty upset. She hates Michele, so you being with her really made the situation worse."

Troy shook his head in frustration. "Thanks, Carol. Will you please tell Sheila that I stopped by again, even though I see her standing in the window in her bedroom upstairs?" He waved at Sheila; she flipped him her middle finger. "Would you tell her that I will not give up on us, and she should just continue to expect calls, texts, and visits from me? Take care Carol."

"You too, Troy." Carol watched Troy drive off. Sheila finally came out of the house with the last bag that belonged to Carol.

"Why did you even entertain him that long? If he and I are through, you should be through with him too."

"Sheila, sometimes you can be so dramatic." Carol laughed.

"Yeah, whatever." Sheila tossed her hair over her shoulder and got into the passenger seat. "I'm glad the kids are at your parents because there is no telling what we might run into at the house you used to share with Jacob once we get over there to get your other stuff."

"All I want is to get clothes and pictures. He can have the furniture and everything else." Carol wiped a tear.

"Are you crying? I can't believe that you are still crying over him."

"I'm not made of ice like you Sheila. I just can't turn my emotions off at will. I don't want Jacob back, but it still hurts me to know that my marriage is over, and the life I once shared with him has really ended. I mean, for God's sake, I have the keys to my own apartment with only my name on the lease, but I'm still legally married."

"Not for long."

"I know, but still the way everything has changed so much in these past months still pains me."

They stood in the driveway talking and feeling the embrace of the beginning of the heat wave for the day.

"Some people go to therapy and talk through their issues, some people rely on their intimacy and relationship with God to see them through and past their hurt and pain, and then there are others like me who bury it deep in the recesses of their mind and move on with life."

"Yeah, and look where your way has gotten you."

"Where, happy?" Sheila laughed.

"If you call the way you've been storming through the house for the past two weeks happy, then I need you to look in the dictionary to look up the real meaning of happiness." Carol smirked and looked at Sheila out of the corner of her eye. She was bracing herself for whatever sarcastic retort Sheila would give her.

"I, you, uh…aw just shut up. You don't know what happiness looks like lately either." They both laughed hysterically.

"Seriously, when are you going to stop ignoring him?"

Sheila raised one eyebrow at Carol. "Maybe never. I don't want to talk about it." Sheila went back to lock her front door.

"Okay." Carol closed the hatch on the back door and got into the driver's side.

Sheila was already buckled up.

Carol started the car up and put the gear into reverse.

"Can we make a detour before we get to your old house?" Sheila stared absentmindedly out of the window.

"Sure," Carol took note of the seriousness in Sheila's tone. "Where to?"

"To my mom's house."

Carol put the car in park. Sheila had not seen or talked to her mother since she was in high school.

There was no need for Sheila to give her the address. Carol's parents had dropped her off there the few times they made Sheila go home when the girls were in high school.

Sheila never let on to Carol or to Carol's parents why she never wanted to go home, but after several times of trying to get answers from Sheila and her mother, they just let things be and let Sheila stay over for as often and for as long as she wanted to.

"Come on, I need to go while I still have the courage to."

# *20*

Carol turned onto Sheila's old street. The pink, tattered two-story house on the corner still served as an eyesore for the block. Old lattice windows, sloping roof, and shutters barely hanging on by one nail distinguished the house and its inhabitants from the rest of the neighbors.

Carol slowly pulled up in front of the house and turned the car off.

The hairs on Sheila's arms stood up. Her eyes glossed over. The silence in the car was eerie.

Carol turned to face Sheila. "Do you want me to go in with you?"

Sheila stared at the house. "No, this is something I have to do on my own." Sheila got out of the car and walked to the front door. She took a deep breath. *You can do this.* She rang the doorbell.

No answer.

She pivoted to walk away, but her feet were cemented to the porch. She took another deep breath. *Be strong.* She knocked.

"Who is it?"

"It's me, Sheila."

Sheila heard shuffling behind the door and the sound of three locks being undone before the door crept open. Wrinkled, deep-set eyes peeped out from the darkness of the hallway. Creased, freckled hands pulled the door wide open.

"Sheila, is that really you?" The woman choked on her tears.

"Yes ma'am."

"Co, come on in." She cleared her throat.

Sheila could not muster up the courage to hug her mother, although she had longed for her touch for so long. She walked into the living room, noting that everything was the exact same way it was the last time she was there over eleven years ago.

She smirked at the dusty pictures of her in two wayward ponytails when she was in the fifth grade and the one of her missing her big front tooth on her first-grade school picture. Her school pictures lined the wall in chronological order.

Her mother stood silently behind her studying Sheila's features. Her hips had widened. The only difference her mother noted was that Sheila's hair was short, close to her head, unlike the shoulder length hair she had growing up. Her mother saw those same gleaming white teeth Sheila always had; along with her alluring round shaped eyes, smooth mocha skin, and that same frown and sadness that Sheila wore as a teenager.

"Do you want something to drink?" Sheila's mother turned and walked towards the kitchen which was at the back of the house.

"No. I can't stay long. I just came to get something off of my chest." Sheila followed her mother to the kitchen.

"I have some pound cake if you want some. It was your favorite when you were a little girl." Sheila's mother reached out to pat Sheila's cheek.

Sheila closed her eyes. She let the calloused hand linger on her face before she took a step back. "Look

Yolanda...ma, I just need to know why?" Sheila inhaled deeply hoping it would suck her tears back in.

"Why what?" Yolanda braced herself on the back of a chair as tears fell down her face.

"Ma-" Sheila heard a creaking sound in the room that was right off the kitchen. The door was open. She slowly walked over to it. Her feet were heavy as she stood in the doorway staring at Uncle Tommy. He laid there in a hospital bed with drool running down the side of his paralyzed face. The room reeked of urine and Lysol.

Sheila smiled. *I'm glad he's suffering now.*

Yolanda walked up behind Sheila and Sheila jumped.

"Sweetie, what's wrong?"

Sheila turned to face her mother. Her eyes narrowed. "You know what's wrong. You let him do those horrible, nasty, and perverted things to me for years, and you never tried to stop it." Sheila wrapped her arms around herself.

"Sheila, baby, sweetheart." Yolanda pulled Sheila towards her. "I swear I didn't find out until after you left."

Sheila pulled away from Yolanda. "How could you not have known ma?"

"I didn't baby, and I'm so sorry. I'm so sorry. I was always working, and overtime at that, trying to get you everything you needed and wanted."

"I didn't need stuff ma. I needed you. I needed you to see what he was doing to me and protect me from him." Sheila huffed and wiped at the streams of tears that flooded her face.

Uncle Tommy's eyes shifted from side to side. He mumbled, but his words were not distinguishable.

"Baby, I know that now, but I didn't know that then. I didn't find out until your senior year when you begged me to let you go live with the Matthews. You're my only child so of course I didn't want you to go live with them, but because I was always at work, and I saw how miserable and depressed you were here, I figured it wouldn't hurt to let you stay with them until you left for college." Yolanda pulled Sheila back closer to her. "Why didn't you tell me?"

Sheila screamed. "Ma, he threatened to hurt me and you so I didn't say anything. After a while, I felt like you knew that it was going on and didn't try to stop it so why should I care about myself if you or he didn't." Her shoulders shrugged as her hands lifted up high in a questioning motion.

Yolanda gripped her stomach and cupped her mouth. She let the weight of what Sheila told her sink in before she spoke. She cupped Sheila's face with both of her hands and searched Sheila's eyes for understanding. "Baby, I swear I had no idea what was going on. It wasn't until after you moved out and the way he kept asking about you that made me question exactly why you left."

Sheila's eyes softened.

"Remember I tried to talk to you several times at the Matthews before you left for college, but you refused to talk to me. I had no way to contact you in college. Even with Edith giving me your number, we still never talked."

Sheila nodded.

"Since you never told me why you left, I decided to ask him if he knew anything seeing as though he was here more than I was. He wouldn't answer me for a while, but something clicked inside of me and after one good night of me and my bat, he confessed."

Sheila's eye widened, and her pupils grew.

"Yes." Yolanda smiled. "There was no need to call the police, only the ambulance. Nobody questioned what happened to him. He was put in an assisted living home because he had brain damage, would never walk again, or be understood when he tries to speak."

"Ma, you didn't."

Yolanda pursed her lips and nodded her head. "Yes, I did. You were my only baby, and I'm so sorry for not being there for you when you needed me the most."

Yolanda opened her arms, and Sheila clothed herself inside of her mother's embrace.

Sheila pulled back to look at her mother. "Why did you take him in if you knew what he did to me?"

"Things aren't always so cookie cutter, Sheila. I hate what he did to you and running you away from here, from me, but when the home called to say they were closing with nowhere to send him and you not having been back here in years…us not talking all of that time, I decided to take him in."

Sheila remained silent.

"It may not seem right to you, but he is my only brother, and he had nowhere else to go. And before you say it, no other home was able to take him in, so I decided too." Yolanda's lips curved down.

Sheila looked back at Uncle Tommy. She looked at her mother then at Tommy again. She walked over closer to his bed.

His eyes widened.

"I have hated you for so long, but I'm tired of carrying around the hurt of what you did to me. Nope, I won't do it anymore." She wiped her eyes and smiled. "I'm choosing freedom and peace over bitterness from now on." She turned to walk back towards her mother. "Ma, I'm sorry for being away all these years. Not speaking to you, holding you just as responsible as him for my pain. I just want to be happy now." Sheila wiped more tears from her face.

"I've always wanted the very best for you and for you to be happy, too." Yolanda wrapped her arms around herself. The tears steadily streamed down her face. "Don't let this be last time I see you again."

"Ma, I've missed you. I want you in my life."

"I can understand if you don't want him here. I can put him out if that means you'll start coming back around." Yolanda laughed. "I'm serious."

"No, you don't have to do that, like you said, he's your brother, but I won't be coming back here again as long as he's here."

Yolanda frowned.

"But that doesn't mean that you can't call me or come visit me whenever you like." Sheila's smile gleamed.

Yolanda pulled Sheila in closely and held on to her as long as she could.

"Ma, I can't breathe." Sheila laughed.

"I'm sorry baby. I've just missed you so much."

"I have to go. Carol is out in the car waiting on me."

They held each other at their waists and walked back towards the front door.

Sheila pulled the front door open.

"Sheila, wait." Yolanda's voice tremored.

"I see your hips have spread, I don't have any grandchildren I've missed out on so far do I?"

Sheila laughed. "No, ma."

"Good." Yolanda exhaled loudly. "But start working on some for me then." She winked.

# *21*

"Jacob, I've told you over and over again that I'm sorry for what happened at little J.J's. birthday party."

Jacob moved past her.

"I'm sorry, but it's over and done with. We can't change the past, but we can build a future together." Michele followed Jacob through the house as he was cleaning up. "What are you doing anyway?"

"What does it look like?"

"Don't get snappy with me! I can see that, but you aren't really cleaning. I can do that for you if you let me." She positioned herself in front of him.

"You just don't get it. Carol is not just some woman, she is my wife that I love, that I want back." Jacob looked away from Michele.

Michele jerked her head back and put her hands on her hips. "You want her back? Why? What about us? What about what we've been doing? The time we've been spending together?"

Jacob rubbed his face with both of his hands in frustration. "She's coming here today to get some more of her and the kids' stuff."

Michele grinned.

"I need you to go before she gets here. You may not know why Carol and I have been separated, but I've been telling you all along that it is just a separation, and I want her back. I'm sorry if you're still not clear about that because we've been sleeping together."

Michele's eyebrows raised. Her eyes narrowed.

"I don't know why I keep going there with you, I just do." He paused. "If Carol were to take me back today, I would stop everything that's been going on between you and me to be with my wife. I'm still in love with her."

"Why? She left you."

"Michele, I just told you where I stand on the matter."

"I thought-"

The doorbell rang interrupting Michele's whining.

***

"Do you know whose car that is?"

"Nope." Carol stood at the front door.

Sheila went to it and looked through the windows. "Mmph, looks like a woman's car to me," Sheila mumbled to herself. "That heifer better not be here." Sheila walked back over to the front door. "Why are you just standing there? Use your key to get in."

"Ice Queen, you make everything sound so simple, but it's not. This was my house, but it's not anymore."

"So. Good riddance to him and this house." Sheila laid on the doorbell ringing it. "Jacob, come open the door now before we let ourselves in."

Jacob soon opened the door.

"Sheila." Jacob acknowledged her.

"Yeah, whatever." Sheila snarled.

"Carol." Jacob softened his voice. He stared at Carol. Even with sweats on, she still was beautiful to him.

Carol pursed her lips. "I-"

Michele came to stand next to him with nothing but one of his old T-shirts on and a sly grin on her face.

Jacob dropped his head in shame. He was so lost staring at Carol the moment earlier that he completely forgot that Michele was there. He cursed under his breath.

Carol stood frozen. She was speechless.

"Carol, let me explain." He clasped his hands as if he was praying.

"You dirty…" Sheila's nostrils flared, and her eyes danced with fire; she was ready to give Jacob and Michele her mind but was interrupted by a process server.

The young man came around Sheila and Carol and stood in front of Jacob. "Jacob Rodgers?"

"Yes." Jacob looked confused.

"You've been served."

# Epilogue

"So, how does it feel to be married?" Carol smiled and sipped on her strawberry lemonade. It was a surprisingly beautiful fall day in Chicago considering the seasons could be so unpredictable. They sat outside of the Italian bistro waiting for their food to be served.

"Great." Sheila beamed.

"I can't believe that you two went to Vegas and eloped."

"Well you better, because we did." Sheila held out her left hand, dropped her wrist, and wiggled her ring finger.

Carol grabbed Sheila's hand. "It's blinding me." Carol covered her eyes.

"Well don't stare directly at it."

They both laughed.

"He did a great job picking out this ring."

Sheila smiled.

"What made you, Sheila 'I'll Never Trust a Man' Collins say 'I Do' to Troy?"

"It's Mrs. all of what you said 'Goodman'. Thank you very much. And he is a good man, in more ways than you'll ever know." Sheila licked her lips and laughed.

Carol scrunched her nose.

"Whatever. Well, confronting my uncle and mother made me realize that I truly wanted to be happy and that could only come from me forgiving him for what he did to me and the role I thought my mother played in the situation."

Sheila read Carol's eyes. "I know I never fully told you what happened when I was younger, but I'll catch you up on that at a later time."

Carol nodded her head.

"So a few days after I helped you get settled at your new place I finally decided to accept a phone call from him. He asked me to meet him for dinner and I did."

Carol's eyebrows raised. She smiled.

"Calm down and let me finish."

Carol laughed.

"I sat there rolling my eyes and smacking my lips while he spoke, as usual."

Carol shook her head at Sheila.

"I felt whole and at peace after seeing my mom. I knew that I really did love Troy, but I didn't want him after he had been in a relationship Michele." A corner of Sheila's lip curled up as she made a hissing sound.

"Stop it." Carol smiled.

"What? You don't care for her either. Any who, I sat there ready to end us once and for all, but he demanded that I shut up so that he could explain some things to me."

Carol put her hand over heart with her mouth gaping open; she pretended to be surprised. "He did not tell Ms. 'Mouth All Mighty' to shut up did he?"

"Oh, you shut up too."

They both laughed.

"He explained that he tried something serious with her, but she detected that he had real feelings for someone else." Sheila leaned in closer to Carol. "He also said something else very interesting."

"What? And why are we whispering when we're the only ones at this table?"

"Oh, you're right." Sheila sat back and laughed.

"He said he thought that she was bipolar!"

Carol's eyes widened.

"Yup, he said she was textbook classic bipolar, and he couldn't handle her kind of crazy anymore."

Carol shook her head. "Well good for him He got out unscathed from her, but you still didn't tell me why you decided to say yes after telling him no all of these years."

"Because, I knew I really do love him and that he was the only man I would ever love and trust. He made that easy for me. When I came to grips with the pain of my past, I knew I wanted love in my present and future. I knew Troy was the only man to give and show me what true love and real intimacy is, so I said yes."

Carol smiled.

"Enough about me, how are you really doing?" Sheila's eyes suggested a more serious tone for Carol.

Carol smiled. "Don't be so solemn, I'm great. It's definitely an adjustment getting up really early to get the kids ready and off to my parents before I head into work. I hate being away from them all day and still having things to do for work at home in the evenings when all I want to do is spend that time with the kids."

"Well at least you have your parents' help and support, some people don't have that."

"True."

"So, what about Eric? Gave him something he can feel yet?" Sheila winked and hummed EnVogue's version of the song.

"No, naughty girl." Carol shook her head at Sheila. "He and I are still just friends and it'll be that way for a looooong time."

"But why? He's such a great guy, and you're not married anymore." Sheila tried to high-five Carol, but Carol would not raise her hand.

"It was a struggle to get Jacob to sign the papers, but once I reminded him of what happened between us this past year and whether or not he wanted those details brought up in court and a possible custody battle, he was quick to sign them."

Sheila smiled.

Carol shook her head. "The ink on my divorce is barely dry, so there will be no dating for me anytime soon. I need to learn more about myself and make sure that I am fully healed from all that I've been through before I even begin to think about a man in that kind of way." Carol twirled her pasta on her fork before she put it up to her mouth.

"Well, I guess that's smart, for you." They laughed. "But I see Jacob didn't waste any time moving on with Michele."

Carol wiped her mouth of marinara sauce. "What do you mean?" Her eyebrows lifted.

"Look over there." Sheila pointed across the street to the tables outside of the pizzeria. "Looks like they are on a date considering that long flowing skirt she has on with her hair pinned up. Doesn't matter how she dresses up, I still say she's a slut."

*** 

"I'm so glad you could meet me here." Michele stared at Jacob.

"What was so urgent that I had to meet you all of a sudden?"

"Look, I just need you to know that I've always loved you, and I'll never stop loving you."

Jacob noted Michele's creepy tone. "Why are you saying it like that?"

"I'm leaving you with full custody of the boys." Michele wiped a tear from her eye.

"What is going on? Are you going somewhere?" Jacob scooted to the edge of his seat. "What have you done?"

Michele's eyes were red, and her tears would not stop falling.

"Michele, what's wrong?"

"I didn't mean for him to die. I swear I didn't mean for him to die." She buried her face in her hands. "I just wanted to cause a small crash that would send him to the hospital with a few stitches. I thought him being in the hospital would bring you and I closer during my time of need." Her words were muffled through her sobs and tears.

Jacob fell back in his seat. His forehead crinkled. "Hunh? What, what are you talking about? What didn't you want to happen? Who are you talking about?"

She lifted her head. Her eyes were blank. "Jacob, they found out that Michael's death wasn't an accident, he was murdered."

Jacob rubbed his head then his knees. He sat upright. "What? Wait, how do you know this?"

"Rita was notified that there would be an investigation into his cause of death before they paid her out the million dollar policy he had."

"Okay, so what does that have to do with what you were talking about?"

"They found out the brakes had been cut and decided the only person that would benefit from his death was his wife, so they arrested her."

Jacob's eyes widened, his mouth gaped open, and he fell back into his chair again. "So you're saying that Rita killed him?"

"No. Haven't you been paying attention? I killed him."

Just then, two detectives walked up to Michele and Jacob's table. Uniformed police officers were behind them.

"Ms. Robinson, we need you to stand up?" The taller of the two detectives spoke.

Michele stood up and smoothed down her skirt, she stepped away from the table.

"Michele, what is going on here?" Jacob jumped up out of his seat.

"Sir, we're going to need you stay back."

"I owed Michael that much. Not to have his wife go down for what I did. Your face is the last face I wanted to see...I love you Jacob."

One of the police officers pulled her hands behind her back to handcuff her. "You have the right to remain silent..."

## Other Books Available

### Sisterhood Chronicles Series
Underneath It All
Discovery
Untold
When It Happens To You
All Things Considered

### Forever Friends Series
Catch Me If You Can
It's Complicated

### Limelight Series
Hues
Tones
Vision

### Standalone Titles
After All Is Said & Done
The Bid Catcher: Distinguished Gentlemen Series

*(Best if you read Forever Friends series before reading Sisterhood Chronicles 3)*

### COMING SOON

The Kissing Game: Love Alive 1

# ABOUT THE AUTHOR

Anita Davis is a former elementary teacher born and raised in Chicago. Although she wrote short stories much of her childhood, she didn't unlock and cultivate her passion as a writer until she became a writing teacher for middle school students. The more she had to create sample writings for her students, the more she realized her passion and ability to tell stories in the written form. She decided to hone her craft as a writer by completing her Master of Fine Arts in Creative Writing via National University. She now pursues writing books most of her time, in addition to being a flight attendant. Anita seeks to encourage, engage, and entertain her readers.

She is Co-Founder of Book Euphoria, a group of Chicago authors bound by their love of literature. Book Euphoria hosts literary events and they also founded the empowerment movement, Black Girl Passion.

Anita writes contemporary romantic women's fiction and seeks to encourage, engage, and entertain her readers.

authoranitadavis@gmail.com
www.authoranitadavis.com
Facebook: Anita Davis and Author page: Author Anita Davis
Instagram: @authoranitadavis    Twitter: @_AnitaDavis